MURDER ON THE THIRTY-FIRST FLOOR

MURDER ON THE
THIRTY-FIRST
FLOOR

(originally titled
The Thirty-First Floor)

Per Wahlöö

*Translated from the Swedish
by Joan Tate*

*Pantheon Books
New York*

All rights reserved under International and Pan-American
Copyright Conventions. Published in the United States by
Pantheon Books, a division of Random House, Inc., New
York, and simultaneously in Canada by Random House of
Canada Limited, Toronto.
First published in Sweden by P. A. Norstedt & Söners Forlag,
Stockholm. Copyright 1964 by Per Wahlöö.
This translation was first published by Michael Joseph
Limited, London, England, under the title *Murder on the
Thirty-First Floor.*

Library of Congress Cataloging in Publication Data

Wahlöö, Per, 1926–1975.
   Murder on the thirty-first floor.
   Reprint. Originally published: The thirty-first floor.
New York: Knopf, 1967, c1966.
   Translation of: Mord på 31: a våningen.
   I. Title.   II. Title: Murder on the 31st floor.
PT9876.33.A35M613   1982   839.7'374   82-47886
ISBN 0-394-70840-7 (pbk.)   AACR2

Manufactured in the United States of America

First American Paperback Edition

To *Maj*

MURDER ON THE
THIRTY-FIRST
FLOOR

I

The alarm was given at exactly 1.02 p.m. The Chief of Police personally telephoned the order down to the Sixteenth Division and ninety seconds later the bells began to ring in the duty room and the offices on the basement floor. They were still ringing when Chief Inspector Jensen came down from his office. Jensen was a middle-aged police officer of average build, with a smooth expressionless face. He stopped on the bottom step of the spiral staircase, let his eyes sweep over the duty room, adjusted his tie and went out to his car.

The midday traffic was thick and glittering and the city buildings rose out of the stream of cars like columns of glass and concrete. In this world of hard surfaces, the people on the sidewalks seemed out of place and unhappy. They were well dressed but strangely alike and every one of them was in a hurry. They milled forward in jerky lines and bunched together at the red lights and chromium-plated express-service counters. They looked around continuously, fingering their briefcases and handbags.

The police vehicles, their sirens wailing, bored their way through the crush.

Inspector Jensen was in the first car, a dark blue standard

vehicle with gilt trimmings; after it came a gray bus with barred windows in the rear door and a rotating light on the roof.

The Chief of Police was speaking from radio headquarters.

"Jensen?"

"Yes."

"Where are you?"

"Immediately opposite the Trade Union Palace."

"Are you using the alarm system?"

"Yes.'

"Cut it out when you've passed the square."

"The traffic is very thick."

"Can't be helped. You must avoid attracting attention."

"The reporters listen to us all the time."

"You needn't bother about that. I'm thinking about the general public. The man in the street."

"I see."

"Are you in uniform?"

"No."

"Good. How many men have you got with you?"

"One, plus four from the Civil Patrol. In the stakeout, nine men from the Order Police. In uniform."

"Only the Civil lot may appear in or immediately outside the building. Let half the stakeout get off three hundred yards before you get there. Then drive on past and park beyond, at a safe distance."

"Right."

"Block the main street and the side streets."

"Right."

"If anyone asks, the road blocks are for urgent road repairs. For instance . . ."

He was silent.

"A burst deep heating pipe?"

"Exactly."

There was a crackle in the receiver.

"Jensen?"

"Yes."

"You know about addressing them?"

"Addressing them?"

"I thought everyone knew. You mustn't call either of them 'sir' ".

"Right."

"They are very sensitive on this point."

"I see."

"I needn't emphasize again the ... er ... delicate nature ... of this assignment?"

"No."

Mechanical noise. Something which could have been a sigh, deep and metallic.

"Where are you now?"

"South side of the square. Opposite the workers' monument."

"Switch off the sirens."

"Done."

"Increase the distance between the vehicles."

"Done."

"I'm sending all available radio patrols as reinforcements. They're heading for the parking lot. Use them as an emergency force."

"Right."

"Where are you?"

"On the north side of the square. I can see the building now."

The street was wide and straight, with six lanes and a narrow white-painted barrier in the middle. Behind a high wire fence along the left side was a slope and below that a long-distance truck depot with hundreds of warehouses and red and white trucks in lines at the loading bays. There were quite a few people about, mostly loaders and drivers in white overalls and red peaked caps.

The street had been dynamited out of a rocky ridge and went uphill. The east side was bordered by a granite wall which had been smoothed over with cement. It was pale blue with perpendicular rust marks on it from iron armatures, and above it a few treetops with bare branches could be seen. From below, it was not possible to see what lay beyond the trees, but Jensen knew both the place and what it looked like. There was a mental hospital there.

At the highest point, the street came level with the ridge and made a slight curve to the right. Just there was the building: it was one of the tallest in the country and, because of its position, could be seen from all parts of the city. One always saw it up above oneself and from whichever direction one came; it seemed to form the terminus of the approach road.

The building was square-based and thirty floors high. On each façade were four hundred and fifty windows and a white clock with red hands. The outer surface was of glazed tiles, dark blue below and getting lighter and lighter the higher they rose.

From Jensen's viewpoint through the car window, the building seemed to shoot up out of the ground like an enormous column growing in the cold cloudless spring sky.

Still holding the radio-telephone to his ear, he leaned

forward. The building became enlarged in his field of vision.

"Jensen?"

"Yes."

"I'm relying on you. It's up to you to size up the situation."

There was a brief crackling pause. Then the Chief of Police said hesitantly:

"End of message."

2

On the eighteenth story, the floors were covered with light blue carpeting. There were also two models of ships there, in glass cases, and a lobby with armchairs and kidney-shaped tables.

Three young women sat idling in a glass-walled room. One of them fleetingly glanced at the visitor and said:

"What's it about?"

"The name's Jensen. It's urgent."

"Oh yes."

She rose indolently and walked across the floor, softly and with studied nonchalance, opened the door and said:

"Someone called Jensen."

Her legs were well shaped and her waist narrow. Her clothes were tasteless.

Another woman appeared in the doorway. She looked a little older, but not much, had blonde hair, clean features and a generally antiseptic air about her.

She looked past her assistant and said at once:

"Come in. You're expected."

The corner room had six windows and below them lay the city, unreal and lifeless, like a model on a topographical map. Despite the sunlight, the view was magnificent and the day clear and cold. The colors in the room were pure and hard and the walls very light, as were the floor covering and the tubular furniture.

Nickel-plated trophies with engraved oak-leaf wreaths on black wooden stands stood in the glass case between the windows. Most of them were topped with naked archers or eagles with their wings outspread.

On the desk was an intercom, a very large stainless steel ashtray and an elegant bone-white telephone.

On top of the glass case stood a red and white table-flag on a chromium stand and under the desk were a pair of light yellow sandals and an empty light metal waste-paper basket.

In the middle of the desk lay a special delivery letter.

There were two men in the room.

One stood at the end of the desk with the tips of his fingers resting on the polished surface. He was dressed in a well pressed dark suit, hand-sewn black shoes, white shirt and a silver-gray silk tie. His face was smooth and servile, his hair well brushed and his eyes dog-like behind the heavy horn-rimmed glasses. Jensen had often seen faces like that, especially on television.

The other man, who looked a little younger, was wearing yellow and white striped socks, light brown trousers and a loose white shirt unbuttoned at the neck. He was kneeling on a chair in front of one of the windows, his chin on his hands and his elbows on the white marble slab. He was fair, blue-eyed and in his stocking feet.

Jensen showed his badge and took a step toward the desk.

"The manager?"

The man in the silk tie shook his head with a parrying

movement and moved away from the desk, bowing slightly with vague eager gestures toward the window. His smile defied analysis.

The fair man slipped from the chair and padded across the floor. He shook Jensen briskly by the hand and then pointed to the desk.

"There," he said.

The envelope was white and of the most ordinary kind. It was franked with three stamps and in the bottom left hand corner was a red special delivery label. In the envelope was a piece of paper, folded twice. Both the address and the contents were composed of letters glued on to the paper, apparently cut from a newspaper. The paper seemed to be of very good quality and of an unusual shape. Jensen held it between the tips of his fingers and read:

> *in retaliation for the murder committed by you a power-ful explosive charge has been placed in the building it is timed and will be detonated at exactly two pm on twenty third march let the innocent save themselves*

"She's mad, of course," the fair man said. "Quite mad."

"Yes, we've come to that conclusion," said the man in the silk tie.

"Or else it's an unusually poor joke," the fair man said. "And tasteless."

"Yes, it could be so," said the man in the silk tie.

The fair man gave him a listless look. Then he said: "This is a director. The managing director."

He paused briefly and added:

"My right-hand man."

The other man's smile broadened and he bowed his

head. He could have been greeting Jensen but he could also have hidden his face for some other reason. Perhaps out of shyness, respect or pride.

"We have ninety-eight other directors," the fair man said.

Jensen looked at his watch. It was 1.19.

"I think you said 'she.' Have you any reason to think that the sender is a woman, sir?"

"No sirs here, I'm just a publisher."

He padded around the desk and sat down, hooking one leg over the arm of the chair.

"No," he said. "Of course not. I just happened to say that, I suppose. Someone must have put the letter together."

"Exactly," said the managing director.

"I wonder who," said the fair man.

"Yes," said the managing director.

His smile had vanished and was replaced by a deep thoughtful frown just above the bridge of his nose.

The publisher hooked his other leg over the arm of the chair.

Jensen looked at the clock. 1.21.

"The building should be evacuated," he said.

"Evacuated? Can't do it. It'd mean our whole production would have to be stopped. Perhaps for a couple of hours. Do you realize what that means? Have you the slightest idea what it'd cost?"

He kicked the swivel-chair around and stared challengingly at his right-hand man. The managing director frowned again and began mumblingly counting his fingers. The man who said he was a publisher looked coldly at him and swung himself back.

"At least a quarter of a million," he said. "Do you see?

A quarter of a million at least. Perhaps double that sum."

Jensen read the letter again and looked at the time. 1.23.

The publisher went on:

"We publish one hundred and forty-four magazines. They are produced in this building. The total number of copies amounts to more than twenty-one million. A week. Nothing is more important than that they be printed and distributed on time."

His expression changed. The blue eyes seemed to clear.

"In every home in this country people are waiting for their magazines. It is the same for all, for princesses at court and the wives of the forestry workers, for the most eminent men and women in the community and for the outcast and degraded, if such people existed, for absolutely everyone."

He stopped for a moment and said:

"And the little children. All the little children."

"Little children?"

"Yes, ninety-eight of our magazines are for children, for the little ones."

"Comics," explained the managing director.

The fair man gave him an ungrateful look and again his expression changed. He kicked the chair around irritably and fastened his eyes on Jensen.

"Well, Inspector."

"With all due respect to those viewpoints, I consider it essential that the building be evacuated," said Jensen.

"Is that all you've got to say? What are your men doing, by the way?"

"Searching."

"If there is a bomb, they should find it, shouldn't they?"

"They know their job, but they haven't much time at their disposal. An explosive charge can be difficult to locate. It might be hidden anywhere. As soon as my men find anything, I'll get a report, here."

"They've still got three quarters of an hour."

Jensen looked at his watch.

"Thirty-five minutes. But even if the charge is found, making it harmless takes quite some time."

"And if there is no bomb?"

"I still must recommend evacuation."

"Even if the risk is insignificant?"

"Yes. The threat perhaps won't be carried out and nothing might happen. But unfortunately there have been instances to the contrary."

"Where?"

"In the criminal records."

Jensen clasped his hands behind his back and rocked to and fro on his heels.

"That's my professional opinion."

The publisher gave him a long look.

"How much would it cost us if your opinion proved to be a different one?" he said.

Jensen looked at him uncomprehendingly.

The man at the desk looked resigned.

"I'm joking, of course," he said gloomily.

He put his legs down, swung the chair back, placed his arms on the desk in front of him and let his forehead drop on to his clenched left fist. Straightened up with a jerk.

"We must consult my cousin," he said, pressing a switch on the intercom.

Jensen checked the time. 1.27.

The man in the silk tie had moved, silently, and was standing close to him. Whispered:

"The boss, the head of the whole concern, the Chief."

The publisher mumbled something into the intercom. Now he pricked up his ears and gave them a cold look. He pressed another button, leaning over the microphone, and spoke, swiftly and business-like:

"House manager? Work out schedule for fire drill. Emergency evacuation. Information to be given in three minutes. Report back for my instructions."

The Chief came into the room. He was fair like his cousin but about ten years older. His face was calm, handsome, and serious, his shoulders broad and he held himself very upright. He was wearing a brown suit, simple and becoming. When he spoke, his voice was deep and resonant.

"The new one; how old is she?" he said absently, with a suggestion of a nod toward the door.

"Sixteen," said his cousin.

"Oh."

The managing director had retired to the glass case, looking as if he were standing on tiptoe, although he was not.

"This man is a policeman," said the publisher. "His men are searching but they've found nothing. He says we must evacuate the place."

The Chief went over to the window and stood still, looking out.

"It's spring already," he said. "How beautiful it is."

It was absolutely silent in the room. Jensen looked at the clock. 1.29.

"Move our cars," the Chief said out of the corner of his mouth.

The managing director dashed to the door.

"They're just beside the building," murmured the Chief. "How beautiful it is."

Thirty seconds' silence.

There was a buzz and a light flickered on the intercom.

"Yes," said the publisher.

"Eighteen to twenty minutes using the staircases, the service elevators and the automatic express elevators."

"Everything included?"

"Not the 31st."

"And the . . . Special Department?"

"Considerably longer time."

The voice on the telephone lost some of its efficiency. "The spiral staircases are narrow."

"I know that."

Click. Silence. 1.31.

Jensen went to one of the windows. A long way down he could see the parking lot and the wide six-lane street, which now lay straight and empty. He also saw that his men had blocked the road with bright yellow trestles about four hundred yards from the building and that one of the men was busy directing the traffic into a side-street. Despite the distance, he could see the policemen's green uniforms and the traffic policeman's white cuffs quite clearly.

Two very large black cars drew out of the lot. They headed south and were followed by another car which was white and presumably belonged to the managing director.

The latter had slunk back into the room and was standing by the wall. His smile was troubled and his head drooped as if he was in profound thought.

"How many floors in the building?" said Jensen.

"Thirty above ground level," said the publisher. "Plus four below. We usually say thirty."

"I thought you mentioned a thirty-first?"

"It was a slip of the tongue."

"How many employees have you?"

"Here? In the building?"

"Yes."

"Four thousand one hundred in the main building. About two thousand in the annex."

"About six thousand altogether then?"

"Yes."

"I maintain they should be evacuated."

The publisher swung a complete circle in his swivel-chair.

The Chief stood with his hands in his pockets and looked out of the window. His clear-cut features were very serious.

"Do you really think there's a bomb in the building?"

"One must in any case reckon with the possibility."

"You are a Chief Inspector?"

"Yes."

"Have you any experience in similar cases?"

Jensen thought for a moment.

"This case is a very special one, but experience shows that statements in anonymous letters in eighty percent of all known cases correspond with reality . . . or are at least based on fact."

"Has that been statistically proved?"

"Yes."

"Do you know what an evacuation would cost us?"

"Yes."

"Our business has struggled against financial difficulties for thirty years. The loss increases year by year. Unfortunately this is a statistical fact. It is only by great personal sacrifices that we have been able to keep going."

His voice had a new ring now, bitter and complaining. Jensen did not reply. 1.34.

"Our activities are wholly idealistic. We are not business men. We are book publishers."

"Book publishers?"

"We look on our magazines as books. They answer the needs which in the past books never succeeded in satisfying."

He looked out of the window.

"Beautiful," he mumbled. "Today when I walked through the park, the first flowers were already out. Snowdrops and aconites. Are you interested in the outdoors?"

"Not especially."

"Everyone should be interested in the outdoors. It would make life richer than ever."

He turned back to Jensen again.

"Do you know what you're asking of us? The price is high. Our position is precarious. Even privately. At home we use large boxes of matches. That's just an example."

"Large boxes of matches?"

"Yes, large, to economize. We have to economize on everything. Large packs are considerably cheaper. It's a sensible economy measure."

The publisher was now sitting on the desk with his feet on the arm of the chair. He looked at his cousin.

"Perhaps it would be a sensible economy measure if there really were a bomb," he said. "The building is beginning to be too small."

The Chief looked at him sadly.

"We're covered by insurance," said the publisher.

"And who covers the insurance company?"

"The banks."

"And the banks?"

The publisher said nothing.

The Chief turned his attention to Jensen.

"I presume you're duty bound not to repeat anything you hear."

"Naturally."

"The Chief of Police recommended you. I hope he knows what he's doing."

Jensen could find no answer to that.

"You haven't put uniformed men inside the building, have you?"

"No."

The publisher pulled his legs up onto the desk and sat cross-legged like a tailor.

Jensen squinted at the clock. 1.36.

"If there's really a bomb here," said the publisher. "Six thousand people . . . tell me, Mr. Jensen, what would the percentage loss be?"

"Percentage loss?"

"Yes, of personnel."

"That's impossible to estimate."

The publisher mumbled, apparently to himself:

"Someone might say we'd let them be blown to bits on purpose. It's a matter of prestige."

"Have you thought about the loss of prestige?" he said to his cousin.

The Chief looked with veiled eyes out over the city, which was white and clean and cubist. Jet planes were drawing patterns of lines across the spring sky.

"Evacuate," he said out of the corner of his mouth.

Jensen noted the time. 1.38.

The publisher put his hand on the intercom and brought his mouth to the receiver. His voice was clear and distinct.

"Fire drill. Emergency evacuation. Within eighteen minutes the building must be empty, with the exception of the Special Department. Begin ninety seconds from . . . now."

The red light went on. The publisher rose and explained:

"It'd be better if the thirty-first floor stayed in the security of their department instead of tramping down the stairs. The current will be cut off as soon as the last elevator reaches the ground floor."

"Who would want to do us such harm?" said the Chief sadly.

He left.

The publisher began to put on his sandals.

Jensen left the room with the managing director.

When the door closed behind them, the corners of the managing director's mouth fell, his expression turned stiff and supercilious, his eyes sharp and watchful. As they went through the secretaries' room, the idle young women seemed to crouch over their desks.

It was exactly 1.40 when Jensen stepped out of the

elevator into the lobby. He made a sign to his men and went through the revolving doors.

The police left the building.

Behind them the voices in the loudspeakers echoed between the concrete walls.

3

The car was parked right up against the cliff wall between the police road-block and the parking lot.

Jensen sat in the front seat by the driver. He was holding a stopwatch in his left hand and the radio microphone in the right. At brief intervals he spoke a few words to the police in the radio cars and at the road-block, gruffly and curtly. He sat upright and the gray hair on the back of his head was thick and short.

In the back sat the man with the silk tie and the changeable smile. His forehead was glistening with sweat and he shifted uncomfortably. Now that neither his superiors nor his subordinates were present, his face had relaxed. His features were slack and apathetic and occasionally his moist pink tongue flickered along his lips. Presumably he had overlooked the fact that Jensen could see him in the driving mirror.

"There's no reason why you should stay here if you find it unpleasant," said Jensen.

"I must. Both the Chief and the publisher have left. That makes me as good as responsible . . . the next in command."

"I see."

"Is there . . . any danger?"

"Practically none."

"But if the whole building collapses?"

"That's highly improbable."

Jensen looked at his stopwatch. 1.51.

Then he looked back at the building. Even from this distance, more than three hundred yards away, it was overpoweringly frightening in its magnificent soaring height and compact weight. The white sunlight was reflected in four hundred and fifty panes of glass, set in identically shaped metal frames, and the blue wall decoration looked smooth, glossy, and cold. It occurred to him that the building could collapse without explosive charges, that the ground could give way beneath its massive weight or the walls could burst from the pressure within them.

An apparently endless stream of people was pouring out of the entrance. It curved in a slow wide loop between the rows of cars in the parking lot, continued through the barred gates in the high wire fencing, down the slope and diagonally across the truck depot's gray concrete yard. Beyond the loading bays and the long packing houses, it dissolved and spread out into a diffuse gray mass, a fog-bank of people. Despite the distance, Jensen noted that about two thirds of the personnel seemed to be women and most of them were dressed in green. Presumably green was this year's spring color.

Two large red vehicles with hoses and collapsible ladders moved out to the parking lot and stopped some distance from the entrance. The firemen sat in rows along the sides and their helmets shone in the sunlight. Not a single sound had come from the sirens or the alarm bells.

By 1.57 the stream of people had thinned out and a

minute later only a trickle of people emerged from the main entrance.

Then there was only one person to be seen, a man, in front of the entrance. When Jensen focussed his eyes, he recognized him. It was the head of the Civil Patrol.

Jensen looked at his stopwatch. 1.59.

Behind him he heard the managing director's nervous movements.

The firemen remained in their seats. The lonely policeman had vanished. The building was empty.

Jensen took a last glance at his stopwatch. Then he stared at the building.

After fifteen, the seconds seemed to stretch out and become longer. Fourteen . . . thirteen . . . twelve . . . eleven . . . ten . . . nine . . . eight . . . seven . . . six . . . five . . . four . . . three . . . two . . . one . . .

"Zero," said Chief Inspector Jensen.

4

"An unprecedented offense," said the Chief of Police.

"But there was no bomb. In fact, nothing happened at all. After an hour, the all-clear for the fire-drill was sounded and the employees went back to work. Before four o'clock everything was back to normal."

"Nevertheless, an unprecedented offense," said the Chief of Police.

His voice was earnest and in some way appealing, as if he were trying to convince not only the person he was talking to, but also himself.

"The offender must be found," he said.

"The investigation is of course proceeding."

"This mustn't be just a routine investigation. You must find the culprit."

"Yes."

"Listen a moment. Naturally I don't want to criticize your methods . . ."

"I did the only possible thing. The risk was too great. It might have been a question of the lives of hundreds of people, perhaps more. If the building had caught fire, we wouldn't have been able to do much. The fire trucks' ladders only reach the seventh or eighth floor. The firemen would have had to work from below and the fire would have worked its way upward all the time. In addition the building is nearly four hundred feet high and the tarpaulins are useless from heights above ninety feet."

"Naturally. I understand all that. And I'm not, as I said, criticizing you. But they're very upset. The break in production is said to have cost them hundreds of thousands. The Chief has been personally in contact with the Minister of the Interior. He did not make any specific complaints."

Pause.

"Thank God," said the Chief of Police. "No specific complaints."

Jensen said nothing.

"But he was very disturbed, as I said. Both about the financial loss and the libelous statement about them. That was his word, libel."

"Yes."

"So the man must be found, immediately."

"It'll take time. The letter is the only lead we've got."

"I know. But the matter must be cleared up."

"Yes."

"The investigation is a delicate one and also, as I said, urgent. From now on you can drop everything else. Consider whatever you've got on hand as inessential."

"I see."

"Today is Monday. You've got a week, no more. Seven days, Jensen."

"I see."

"You must do this yourself. Naturally you'll have all the technical staff at your disposal, but don't tell them about the case. If you need advice, come directly to me."

"I must stress that the men in the Civil Patrol already know something about it."

"Yes, that's most unfortunate. You must swear them to absolute secrecy on the matter."

"Of course."

"You yourself must undertake all essential interrogations."

"Right."

"One more thing. They don't want to be disturbed by the investigation. Their time is extremely limited. Whatever information you consider necessary to have, they prefer you to get through their executive head, the managing director."

"I see."

"You've already met him?"

"Yes."

"Jensen?"

"Yes."

"You must succeed. Not least for your own sake."

Jensen put down the receiver. He propped his elbows on the green blotter and his head on his hands. The short gray hair felt stiff on the tips of his fingers. He had begun his spell of duty fifteen hours earlier, it was ten o'clock at night and he was very tired.

He rose from his desk, stretched, went out into the corridor and on down the spiral staircase into the duty room. It was equipped in the same old-fashioned way and painted the same pale green as it had been in the days when he had been a patrol constable twenty-five years earlier. A long wooden counter ran across the room and behind it were benches along the walls and a row of interrogation rooms with glass panes and wooden door-knobs. At this time not many people were there. A few drunks and starving prostitutes, all middle-aged or older, were squatting on the benches waiting their turn in the interrogation rooms, and behind the counter sat a police man in a green linen uniform on telephone duty. Now and again the sounds of cars thundered in through the entrance.

Jensen opened the steel door in the wall and went down into the basement. The Sixteenth Division's station was old, almost the only old one left in this part of the city, rather poorly maintained, but the cells were newly built. The ceilings, floors and walls were painted white and the grids shone in the sharp etching light.

A gray police bus was standing at the entrance to the yard with its rear doors open. A few uniformed police were hustling a bunch of drunks in for examination. They dealt with them roughly, but Jensen knew that this was due more to fatigue than to brutality.

He went through to the examination room and looked at the naked despairing faces of the drunks.

Although it was severely denounced, public drunken-ness was on the increase every year, and since the govern-ment had passed a new law forbidding drunkenness even in the home, the volume of work put on the police had become almost inhuman. Every night, between two and three thousand more or less incapably inebriated people were arrested, about half of them women. Jensen remem-bered his time as patrol officer when three hundred drunks on a Saturday night would have been considered a very large number.

An ambulance had driven up alongside the bus and behind it stood a young man in a sports cap and a white coat. He was the police doctor.

"Five who had to go to hospital for stomach pumping," he said. "I don't dare keep them here. Can't take the responsibility."

Jensen nodded.

"It's a damn mess," said the police doctor. "They put a five thousand percent tax on spirits. Then they create a society which forces people to drink themselves to death, and to crown everything they collect sixty thousand dollars a day in fines for drunkenness, here in the city alone."

"You should watch your tongue," said Chief Inspector Jensen.

5

Jensen lived in a relatively central residential area on the south side of the city, and it took him less than an hour to drive there in the police car.

In the center of the city itself, the streets were fairly crowded, the self-service counters and the movie houses still open and a number of people were moving on the sidewalks along the rows of illuminated shop windows. Their faces looked tense and white, as if tormented by the cold white light from the street lamps and the glare from advertisements. Here and there idle groups of youngsters were gathered around the popcorn stalls or in front of shop windows. They were mostly standing still, apparently hardly speaking to each other at all. Some of them glanced indifferently at the police car.

Juvenile delinquency, which had formerly been considered a serious problem, had steadily declined during the last ten years and now had been practically eradicated. On the whole, there was less crime than before; only drunkenness had increased. At several places in the business section of the city, Jensen saw uniformed constables at work. Their white rubber truncheons flashed in the neon light as they hustled the arrested people into the police buses.

He drove down into the motor tunnel by the Ministry of the Interior and came out five miles farther on in a deserted industrial area. Then he crossed a bridge and continued south on the highway.

He was tired, and he had an ache in the right side of his diaphragm, a heavy, grinding pain.

The suburb in which he lived consisted of thirty-six eight-story blocks arranged in four parallel rows. Between them were parking lots, lawns and play-houses of transparent plastic for the children.

Jensen stopped outside the seventh block in the third row, switched off the ignition and got out into the cold starry night. Although it was only five past eleven, no lights were on in the building. He dropped a coin into the parking meter, twisted the handle with the time-indicator and went up to his apartment.

He switched on the light and took off his shoes, tie and jacket. He unbuttoned his shirt and walked through the apartment, glancing at the impersonal furniture, the large television set and the photographs from the police college hanging on the walls.

Then he drew the blinds, took off his trousers and put the light out. He went into the kitchen and took the bottle out of the refrigerator.

Jensen got a glass, folded back the spread and the top sheet and sat down on his bed.

He sat in the dark and drank.

When the ache in his stomach had gone, he put the glass on the bedside table and went to bed.

He fell asleep almost at once.

6

Jensen woke at half-past six in the morning. He got out of bed and went into the bathroom, washed his hands, face and neck with cold water, shaved and brushed his teeth. When he had gargled, he coughed for a long time.

Then he boiled some honey-water and tried to drink it as hot as possible while he was reading the newspapers. Not one of them mentioned the events he had been involved in the previous day.

The traffic on the highway was heavy and although he used his siren, it was twenty-five to nine when he arrived at his office.

Ten minutes later, the Chief of Police called.

"Have you started the investigation?"

"Yes."

"Along what lines?"

"The material evidence is being analyzed. The psychologists are examining the text. A man is working on the post-office angle."

"Any results?"

"Not yet."

"Have you personally any theory?"

"No."

Silence.

"My background knowledge of the enterprise is inadequate," said Jensen.

"It'd be a good thing to refresh your memory."

"Yes."

"Even better to get your information from some source outside the concern."

"I see."

"I suggest the Ministry of Communications, perhaps the Secretary of State for Publicity."

"I see."

"Do you usually read their magazines?"

"No, but I shall."

"Good. And for God's sake stop annoying the publisher and his cousin."

"Would there be any objection if I have Civil Patrol men acting as bodyguards?"

"To the two bosses?"

"Yes."

"Without their knowledge?"

"Yes."

"Do you consider such a measure justified?"

"Yes."

"Do you think your men can get away with it?"

"Yes."

The silence that followed went on so long that Jensen began to look at the clock. He heard the Chief of Police breathing and tapping on his desk with something, presumably a pen.

"Jensen?"

"Yes."

"From now on the investigation is entirely in your

hands. I don't want to be informed about your methods or about the measures you take."

"I see."

"The responsibility is yours. I am relying on you."

"I see."

"The general directive for the investigation is quite clear?"

"Yes."

"Good luck."

Jensen went out to the cloakroom, filled a paper cup with water and returned to his desk. He pulled out a drawer and took out a bag of bicarbonate, poured out about three teaspoons of the white powder and stirred it with his plastic pen.

During his twenty-five years' service in the corps, he had seen the Chief of Police only once and had never spoken to him until the day before. Since then they had had five conversations.

He emptied the cup in one gulp, crumpled it up and flung it into the waste-paper basket. Then he called the Criminal Technical Institute. The laboratory man's voice was dry and formal.

"No, no fingerprints."

"Are you sure?"

"Naturally. But nothing is definite. We are trying other methods."

"The envelope?"

"One of the most common types. So far tells us very little."

"And the paper?"

"That seems to be special. And it also looks as if it has been torn along one edge."

"Can it be traced?"

"Possibly."

"Anything else?"

"Nothing. We're working on it."

He put down the receiver, went over to the window and looked down to the concrete yard of the police station. At the entrance to the cells, he could see two policemen in rubber boots and waterproof overalls. They were dragging out the hoses to swill down the cells. He loosened his belt and swallowed air until the gasses in his stomach were forced up to his throat.

The telephone rang. It was the man at the post office.

"This is going to take some time."

"Take the time you need, but no more."

"How often shall I report back?"

"Every morning at eight o'clock, in writing."

Jensen put down the receiver, picked up his hat and left the room.

The Ministry of Communications lay right in the center of the city, between the Royal Palace and the central office of the Combined Parties. The Secretary of State for Publicity had his office on the second floor, with a view facing the palace.

"The company is a model of good administration," he said. "A credit to free enterprise."

"I see."

"I can probably help you best with some statistical information."

He picked up a file and leafed absently through it.

"They publish one hundred forty-four different magazines. Last year the total net issues amounted to twenty-one million, three hundred twenty-six thousand, four hundred fifty-three copies. A week."

Jensen noted down the number on a little white card. 21,326,453.

"That's a very large number. It signifies that our country has the highest reading-frequency in the world."

"Are there no other weeklies?"

"A few. About a thousand or so copies altogether are printed and distributed only within very limited areas."

Jensen nodded.

"But the company is, of course, only *one* branch of the concern."

"Which are the others?"

"In my department's jurisdiction, there is a chain of printing companies which mainly produce newspapers."

"How many?"

"Companies? Thirty-six."

"And how many newspapers?"

"A hundred or so. One moment . . ."

He consulted his papers.

"One hundred two at the moment. The publication of newspapers is constantly fluctuating. Some papers close down, others take their place."

"Why?"

"To meet new demands and follow the trends of the times."

Jensen nodded.

"The net publication of daily papers last year . . ."

"Yes?"

"I have only the figure for the total newspaper production in the whole country. Nine million, two hundred sixty-five thousand, three hundred twelve copies per day. It's the same in this case. There are also one or two papers printed which are independent of the concern. They suffer from distribution difficulties and their circulation is very insignificant. If you lower the figure I gave you by about five thousand, you'd get roughly the right figure."

Jensen again wrote on the little white card. 9,260,000. He said:

"Who controls the distribution?"

"A democratic combine of newspaper publishers."

"All of them?"

"Yes, with the limitation that their papers must be printed in editions of over fifty thousand copies."

"Why?"

"Smaller editions are not considered profitable. In fact the concern stops publishing papers whose numbers fall below the figure I have just mentioned."

Jensen put the card in his pocket.

"In practice then, this means that the concern controls all the publications in the country, doesn't it?"

"If you like to put it that way. But I must point out that their publications are very varied, praiseworthy from all points of view. The weekly magazines in particular have proved their ability to satisfy in a moderate way all legitimate tastes. Before, the press often had an inflammatory effect on the readers. That is not the case any longer. Now the content and form is aimed entirely at both the reader's benefit . . ."

He glanced down at the file and turned over a page.

". . . and enjoyment. They are aimed at the family, to be readable at all levels, not to create aggressions, unhappiness, or anxiety. They satisfy the ordinary person's need for escapism. Briefly, they promote social equality."

"I see."

"Before the final solution on social equality, the publication of magazines and papers was much more diffuse than now. The political parties and the trades unions each had their own publishing companies. But when they got into financial difficulties, they either closed down or were taken over by the concern. Many of them were thanks to . . ."

"Yes?"

"Thanks to those very principles I've just mentioned. Thanks to their capacity to give peace of mind and security to the readers. The ability to be comprehensible and uncomplicated, adapting to the tastes of modern man."

Jensen nodded.

"I don't think it is an exaggeration to state that a united press has, more than anything else, contributed to consolidating social equality. To bridging the gap between political parties, between monarchy and republic, between the so-called upper class and . . ."

He fell silent and looked out of the window. He continued:

"Neither is it an exaggeration to say that great praise is due to the leaders of the concern. Excellent men of high . . . moral character. Quite without vanity, striving neither for position, nor power, nor . . ."

"Wealth?"

The Secretary of State threw a swift questioning look at the man in the visitor's chair.

"Exactly," he said.

"What other companies are controlled by the concern?"

"Heaven only knows," said the Secretary of State absentmindedly. "Distribution companies, packaging companies, shipping, furniture-making, the paper industry, of course, and . . . that's not my department."

He fixed his eyes on Jensen.

"I don't think I can give you any more useful information," he said. "Anyhow, why all this interest?"

"Orders," said Jensen.

"To change the subject, how has the increase in authority given to the police affected the statistics?"

"Of the suicide rate?"

"Exactly."

"Positive."

"Delighted to hear it."

Jensen put four more questions.

"Don't the activities of the concern come up against the anti-trust laws?"

"I'm not a lawyer."

"What's the concern's turnover?"

"That's the tax authority's affair."

"And the owners' private fortune?"

"Could hardly be calculated."

"Were you employed in the concern?"

"Yes."

On his way back, he stopped at a cafeteria and drank a cup of tea and ate two rye biscuits.

While he did so, he thought about the suicide figures, which had markedly improved since the passing of the new laws on the abuse of alcohol. The institutions for alcoholics issued no statistics and suicides at police stations were registered as sudden death. Despite careful examination, they still occurred quite often.

When he returned to the Sixteenth Division, it was already two o'clock and the drunks were pouring in. That this had not happened earlier was because arrests were not usually made before midday. This general decision was considered to have been made in the interests of hygiene, to give time for the cells to be disinfected.

The police doctor was smoking in the guard room, one elbow resting on the wooden counter. His white coat was crumpled and blood-stained and Jensen looked at it critically. The other man misunderstood his look and said:

"Nothing serious. Only some poor devil who ... He's dead now. I got there too late."

Jensen nodded.

The doctor's eyelids were swollen and inflamed, with small lumps of pus stuck to the eyelashes.

He looked thoughtfully at Jensen and said:

"Is it true, as I've heard, that you've never failed on a case?"

"Yes," said Jensen. "That's right."

7

On the table in his office lay the magazines he had asked for. One hundred forty-four of them, arranged in four heaps with thirty-six in each.

Jensen drank a cup of bicarbonate and let his belt out yet another hole. Then he sat down at his desk and began to read.

The production of the magazines varied slightly in shape, format and number of pages. Some of them were printed on glossy paper, some not. A comparison indicated that this seemed to determine the price.

All had colored pictures on the front cover, portraying cowboy heroes, supermen, members of the royal family, pop-singers, television stars, famous politicians, children and animals. Children and animals were often featured in the same pictures in different combinations, for instance small girls with kittens, small blond boys with puppies, small boys with very large dogs and almost fully-grown girls with very small cats. The people on the covers were beautiful, blue-eyed, and had smooth friendly faces. This was true of the children and animals too. When he took out his magnifying glass and looked closely, he noticed that the faces had strange lifeless patches, as if something had been removed from the photographs, perhaps moles, pore-marks or bruises.

Jensen read the magazines as if they were reports, swiftly but thoroughly and without skipping anything except for what he already knew. After an hour or so he noticed that such bits recurred more and more often.

At half-past twelve he had finished seventy-two magazines, exactly half. He went down to the duty room, exchanged a few words with the man on telephone duty and drank a cup of tea in the canteen. Despite the steel doors and the thick brick walls, the sound of wild cries and frightened yelps penetrated up from the basement. As he was returning to his room, he noticed that the policeman in the green linen uniform was reading one of the magazines he himself had been studying. Three more lay on the shelf below the counter.

It took him only a third of the time to go through the second half of the publications. It was twenty to three when he turned the last glossy page and looked at the last friendly face.

He ran the tips of his fingers lightly down his cheeks and verified that his skin felt tired and flabby under the stubble. He was not especially sleepy and was still suffering sufficient pain from the tea not to feel hungry.

He drooped a bit, leaned his left elbow on the arm of the chair and let his cheek rest against the palm of his hand as he gazed at the magazines.

He had read nothing that had interested him and at the same time nothing that he had found unpleasant, disturbing, or unsympathetic. Nor anything that had made him pleased, angry, sad or surprised. He had been given access to a considerable amount of information, mostly on cars and different people in prominent positions, but none of this information was of such a nature that it might influence anyone's attitude or way of thinking. Criticism was directed almost entirely at unknown historical psychopaths, in exceptional cases in far distant countries, and then always in vague and very polite tones.

A number of questions were discussed, usually appearances on television programs on which someone had sworn or been unshaven or had untidy hair. These matters were treated by the magazines in a spirit of conciliation and understanding, which clearly indicated that all the parties were right. These conclusions seemed mostly obvious.

A great deal of the content consisted of stories and was presented as such with colorful, realistic illustrations. Like the factual material, they were about people who had enjoyed success in entertainment and business. Their form was not always the same, but as far as he could make out, they were neither more nor less complicated, whether in the big glossy magazines or in the comic strips.

He noticed that the magazines were aimed at different classes of society, but the content was always the same, the same people praised, the same stories told. Although the style varied, the general impression was that they had all been written by the same person.

It seemed preposterous that anyone could take offense or be seriously disturbed by what was in these magazines. The writers did often go quite deeply into personalities, but the excellence and high moral caliber of the people mentioned were never questioned. Naturally it was possible that some people who had succeeded in life were not mentioned or were mentioned less than others, but that was a doubtful clue and in addition seemed highly improbable.

Jensen took out his little white card from his breast pocket and wrote down very neatly: 144 magazines. No clues.

On his way home, he found he was hungry and he stopped at an automat. He bought two sandwiches wrapped in plastic and ate them as he drove.

By the time he arrived, he already had a sharp pain on the right side of his diaphragm.

He undressed in the dark and got the bottle and the glass. He turned back the spread and the sheet and sat down on his bed.

8

"I want a report every morning before nine o'clock. In writing. Everything they think important."

The head of the Civil Patrol nodded and left.

It was Wednesday and the time was two minutes past nine. Jensen went to the window and looked down at the overalled men, busy with their hoses and buckets of disinfectant.

He returned to his desk, sat down, and read the reports. Two of them were very brief.

The man at the post office:

The letter was mailed in the western section of the city, no earlier than nine o'clock on Sunday night, no later than ten o'clock on Monday morning.

The laboratory:

The analysis of the paper has been completed. White, wood-free paper of high quality. Place of manufacture still unknown. Type of glue: Ordinary office glue, film dissolved in acetone. Manufacture: Indefinite.

The psychologist:

It can be presumed that the person who composed the letter either has a pronouncedly rigid character or is of a depressive nature, possibly with compulsive inclinations.

It would not under any circumstances be a matter of a flexible personality. In any case, it can definitely be said that the person in question is thorough, bordering on pedantry or perfectionism, and in addition the person in question is used to expressing himself, either in speech or writing, probably the latter, and almost certainly has been so for a considerable period of time. Great care has been taken over the actual construction of the letter, both technically and from a contents angle, e.g. the choice of type (all letters the same size) and the very even arrangement. Indicates rigidity and lack of flexibility of mind, as is often the case. Certain details of the choice of words point to the fact that the writer is a man, probably not very young, and something of an odd man out. None of these viewpoints is sufficiently substantiated to be considered definite, but they eventually may give a lead.

The report was typed, unevenly and carelessly with a great many faults and erasures.

Jensen carefully punched holes in the three reports and placed them in a green file on the left of his desk. Then he rose, picked up his hat and coat and left the room.

The weather was still beautiful. The sunlight was sharp and bright but not very warming, the sky ice-blue, and in spite of the gas fumes, the air seemed clear and pure. People who had temporarily got out of their cars could be seen on the sidewalks. As usual, they were well dressed and looked alike. They moved swiftly and nervously, as if longing to be back in their cars. Once inside them, their sense of integrity was strengthened. As the cars were in themselves different, in color, size, shape and horsepower, they gave their owners a sense of identity. In addition, they brought about a division into groups; people with similar cars unconsciously felt a sense of belonging to a category of equals which was more apparent than the egalitarian society as a whole.

Jensen had read this in a report from the Ministry of Social Matters. It had been written by several state psychologists and circulated to the senior police officers. After that it had been scheduled top secret.

When he found himself on the south side of the square, immediately opposite the workers' monument, he saw in the car mirror an identical police car to his own. He thought it was occupied by a Chief Inspector from one of the neighboring divisions, presumably Fifteenth or Seventeeth.

As he drove toward the building, he listened absently to the short-wave receiver, which at brief intervals sent out short cryptic messages from headquarters to the stake-outs and patrol cars. He knew that the crime reporters on the daily papers had permission to listen in on this radio traffic. With the exception of road accidents, however, practically nothing sensational or disturbing ever happened.

He drove to the parking lot and left his car between the two large black cars and the managing director's white one.

An attendant in white uniform and a red peaked cap came up to him immediately. Jensen showed his badge and went into the building.

The express elevator stopped automatically at the eighteenth floor and not once on the way up, but nearly twenty minutes elapsed before he was shown in. He passed the time by studying the models of the two liners which had been named after the Prime Minister and His Majesty the King.

He was shown in by a blank-eyed woman secretary in a green suit. The room was identical to the one he had been in two days earlier, except that the trophies in the glass case were somewhat smaller and the view through the window different.

The managing director stopped polishing his nails for a moment and offered him a chair.

"Is the matter already cleared up?"

"Unfortunately not."

"Should you require assistance or information I have orders to give you every possible help. I am at your service."

Jensen nodded.

"Though I must warn you I am exceptionally busy."

Jensen looked at the trophies and said:

"Were you a sportsman?"

"I'm an outdoor man. Still active. Sailing, fishing, archery, golf . . . Of course, not in the same class as . . ."

He smiled timidly and made a vague gesture toward the door. A few seconds later the corners of his mouth fell again. He looked at his watch, a large and elegant one with a broad gold-link strap.

"In what way can I help you?"

Jensen had long since formulated the questions he had come to ask.

"Has anything ever happened which might give a plausible explanation for the expression 'the murder committed by you'?"

"Of course not."

"You can't explain it, connect it with anyone or anything?"

"No, as I said, of course not. A madman's fantasies. A madman, that's the only possible explanation."

"There have not been any deaths?"

"Certainly not recently. But on that point, I suggest you turn to the personnel manager. I am really a journalist, responsible for the contents of our papers and their editorial production. And . . ."

"Yes?"

"And in any case, you're on quite the wrong track. Don't you see how absurd the idea is?"

"What idea?"

The man in the silk tie looked irresolutely at his visitor.

"One more question," said Jensen. "If we presume that the object of the letter was to persecute the heads of the company, or one of them—within which category do you think the guilty man can be found?"

"That's for the police to decide. I've already made up my mind. Among the mentally sick."

"Are there no single individuals or any special group who might feel ill-will toward the company or its heads?"

"Do you know our publications?"

"I have read them."

"Then you should know that the whole of our policy is directed at exactly that; not to create ill-will, aggressions or differences of opinion. Our publications are healthy and enjoyable. Least of all do they aim at complicating the lives and emotions of our readers."

The man paused briefly, and said conclusively:

"The company has no enemies. Neither have the heads. The idea is preposterous."

Jensen was sitting upright and motionless in the visitor's chair. His face was utterly expressionless.

"It's possible that I shall be forced to make certain investigations in the building."

"In that case you must be absolutely discreet," the managing director said at once. "Only the Chief, his cousin and myself know about your assignment. Naturally we'll do everything to help you, but I must point out that under no circumstances must it become known that the police are taking an interest in the company, least of all by the employees."

"Investigation demands a certain amount of freedom of movement."

The man thought. Then he said:

"I can give you a master-key and an identity card which will give you access to the different departments."

"Yes."

"That would, so to speak . . . justify your presence."

The managing director drummed on the edge of his desk with his fingers. Then he smiled, affably and secretively, and said:

"I shall personally formulate and write this document. Perhaps that'd be best."

As if in passing, he pressed a button beside his intercom and a panel with a typewriter on it slid out from the side of the desk. The typewriter was streamlined and shone with chromium-plate and lacquer and there was nothing to indicate that it had ever been used.

The managing director opened one of the drawers and took out a little blue card. Then he swung around in his swivel-chair, nipped lightly at his jacket sleeves and carefully put the card into the typewriter. He manipulated the machine for a moment, thoughtfully rubbed his nose with his forefinger, hit some of the keys, pushed his glasses up on his forehead and gazed at what he had written, drew the card out of the typewriter, crumpled it up, threw it into the waste-paper basket and took another one out of the drawer.

He put it in and typed slowly. After each blow, he pushed up his glasses and looked at the result.

When he had crumpled up the card, his smile was no longer quite so affable.

He took yet another out of the drawer. The next time, he took five.

Jensen was sitting upright and immobile and seemed to be looking past him, at the glass case, the cups, and the miniature flag.

After the seventh card, the managing director had given up smiling. He unbuttoned his collar and loosened his tie, took a black fountain-pen with a silver monogram on it out of his breast pocket and began to write rough drafts on a sheet of discreetly headed notepaper.

Jensen said nothing and his gaze did not falter.

A drop of sweat rolled down the managing director's nose and fell onto the paper.

The man seemed to start and wrote swiftly and scratchily. Then he crumpled the paper up violently and threw it under the desk. It missed the aluminium waste-paper basket and landed at Jensen's feet.

The managing director rose and went across to one of the picture windows, opened it and stood there with his back to his visitor.

Jensen glanced at the paper, picked it up and put it in his pocket.

The managing director shut the window and came smiling across the floor. He buttoned up his collar, pulled up his tie and made the typewriter vanish. He put his finger on the intercom and said:

"Write out a temporary employment card for a Mr. Jensen, giving him free access within the building. He's part of the building inspectorate. Valid until Sunday. Get me a master-key."

His voice was hard and cold and imperious, but his smile remained unchanged.

Exactly ninety seconds later, the woman in green brought in the document and the key. The managing director's face fell, he looked critically at the card and said with a slight shrug:

"Oh well, it'll do."

The secretary's eyes wavered.

"I said it'd do," said the managing director sharply. "So you can go."

He scribbled his signature on it, handed the card and the key to his visitor and said:

"The key fits all departments which would be of interest to you. Of course, not the private rooms, nor this one."

"Thank you."

"Have you any more questions? If not then . . ."

He looked regretfully at his watch.

"Just one minor point," said Jensen. "What is the Special Department?"

"A project group working on the plans for new magazines."

Jensen nodded, put the key and the blue card into his breast pocket and left the room.

Before starting the car, he took out the crumpled sheet

of paper, smoothed it out and felt it carefully with the tips of his fingers. It seemed to be very good quality and the shape was unusual.

The managing director's handwriting was as uneven and jagged as a child's, but was not difficult to make out. Jensen read:

Building inspector herewith
Mr. N. Jensen belongs to the inspection indoors and is granted permission to all departments except
N. Jensen is a member of the building inspectorate and has right departments
Mr. Jensen, bearer of this card, is herewith allowed admission to the concerns'
N. Jensen belongs to the building inspectorate and special authorities
Commissioner. Commissioner.
Mr. Jensen BLAST FUCK HELL

He folded the sheet of paper and put it in the glove compartment on top of his service revolver. Then he leaned his head against the car window and looked up at the building, his eyes calm and vacant.

His stomach churned. He was hungry but knew that he would soon be in pain if he ate anything.

Jensen switched on the ignition and looked at his watch. It was half-past twelve and already Wednesday.

9

"No," said the laboratory man, "it's not the same kind of paper. Nor the same shape. But . . ."

"But?"

"The difference in quality is not very great. The structure is similar. Anyhow, fairly unusual."

"And?"

"It's not beyond the bounds of possibility that both bits of paper were made in the same factory."

"Oh yes."

"We're checking now. It's a possibility, anyhow."

The man seemed to hesitate. After a moment, he said:

"Has the man who wrote the sentences on this bit of paper anything to do with the case?"

"Why do you ask?"

"A man from the Criminal Psychiatric Institute who was here had a look at it. He concluded that whoever wrote the text suffers from word-blindness. He was pretty definite on that point."

"Who gave this psychiatrist the opportunity to see the material?"

"I did. I happen to know him. He came here quite by chance."

"I'll report you for dereliction of duty."

Jensen put down the receiver.

"Pretty definite," he said to himself.

"Fairly unusual," he said.

He went out to the cloakroom, got a mug of water, poured out three teaspoonsful of bicarbonate, stirred it with his pen and drank.

He took out the key. It was flat and long and the complicated head was a strange shape. He weighed the key in his hand and glanced at the clock.

It was twenty past three and it was still Wednesday.

From the vestibule, Jensen turned left and took the service elevator below ground. The articulated framework of the elevator cages creaked slowly downward and he noted attentively what there was to be seen on the different floor levels. First came a very large hall where electric trucks were moving along narrow passages between newly packed magazines, then overalled men with piled-up molds on trolleys and then the deafening racket from the rotary-presses. On the next floor he saw a shower-room, basins, cloakrooms with benches and rows of green steel lockers. On the benches sat people who were evidently having a break or had finished their shift. Most of them were leafing apathetically through colored magazines which had presumably just come off the press. Then his trip came to an end and he stepped out to find himself in the paper store room. It was quiet down there, but not completely so, for the accumulated sounds from the immense building above penetrated down like a great pulsating roar. For a while he walked around aimlessly between rows of bales and upright rolls of paper. The only person he saw was a small pale man in a white coat, who stared in terror at him and crushed out his cigarette in his clenched fist.

Jensen left the store room and rode up. On the street level he was joined by a middle-aged man in a gray suit. The man stepped into the same compartment and went with Jensen as far as the tenth floor, where they had to change. He said nothing and at no time looked at his fellow-passenger. In the service elevator from the tenth floor, Jensen discovered that the man in the gray suit had got into the compartment below his own.

At the twentieth floor, he crossed to a third service elevator and four minutes later he was at the top.

He found himself in a narrow, windowless, uncarpeted concrete corridor. It ran in a square around a kernel of the stairway and elevators, and along its outer sides were white-painted doors. To the left of each door was a little notice on which stood one, two, three or four names. The corridor was flooded with cold blue-white light from the strip lights in the ceiling.

From the notices it appeared that he was in the comic strip magazine editorial department. He walked down five flights of stairs and found himself still in the same department. There were very few people in the corridors but he could hear voices and the clatter of typewriters through the doors. On each floor there was a bulletin board on which were notices mainly from the executives of the firm to the employees. There were also time-clocks, control clocks for the night-watchman and, in the ceiling, an automatic sprinker system.

On the twenty-fourth floor, there were four different offices. He recognized the names of the magazines and remembered that they were all simply produced and mostly contained stories with color illustrations.

Jensen worked his way slowly downward. On each floor

he walked along four corridors, two longer and two shorter, joined into a rectangle. The doors were painted white here too, and the walls were bare. With the exception of the names on the doors, the seven top floors were identical. Everything was very well cared for, there was no sign of slovenliness and the cleaning seemed irreproachable. Behind the doors could be heard voices, telephones ringing and here and there the sound of typewriters.

He stopped by one of the bulletin boards and read:

Do not talk disparagingly of the Company or its magazines! It is forbidden to fasten pictures or articles of any kind whatsoever on the outside of the doors!
Always act as an ambassador for the Company. In your free time too! Remember that the Company acts as is fitting; with discrimination, dignity and responsibility! Counteract unjustified criticism. "Escape from reality" and "hypocrisy" are just other names for poetry and imagination!
Always be conscious of the fact that you represent the Company and your magazine! In your free time too!
"True" reporting is not always the best! "The truth" is a commodity which must be handled with utmost caution in modern journalism. You cannot be sure that everyone will tolerate it as well as you can!
Your task is to entertain our readers, to stimulate them to dream. Your task is not to shock, excite or disurb, nor is it to "awaken" or educate.

There were several other notices of a similar nature. Most of them were signed by execuitves of the company or those in charge of the building, only a few by the publisher personally. Jensen read them all, then continued downward.

The larger and more elegant magazines were evidently

produced farther down the building. The interior decoration was somewhat different there, with light carpets in the corridors, tubular chairs and chromium ashtrays. The nearer he got to the eighteenth floor, the more the chilly elegance increased, and after that it decreased again. The directors' department took up four floors, farther down were offices for administration, advertising and distribution and much else. The corridors again became bare and white and the clatter from typewriters intensified. The light was cold, white, and very bright.

Jensen went through floor after floor. When he reached the big vestibule it was nearly five o'clock. He had used the stairs all the way and perceived a vague feeling of fatigue at the back of his knees and in his calves.

About two minutes later the man in the gray suit came down the stairs. Jensen had not seen him since they had parted at the service elevator on the tenth floor an hour earlier. The man went into the commissionaire's cubbyhole by the main entrance. He could be seen saying something to the uniformed man behind the glass wall. Then he wiped the sweat from his forehead and threw a fleeting, uninterested glance over the vestibule.

The clock in the great hall struck five and exactly a minute later the automatic doors of the first loaded express elevator opened.

The stream of people continued for more than half an hour before it began to thin out. Jensen stood with his hands clasped behind his back and slowly rocked backward and forward on the soles of his feet as he watched people hurrying by. Beyond the revolving doors, they scattered and disappeared toward their cars, meek and bent.

At a quarter to six the vestibule was empty. The elevators were still. The men in white uniforms locked the entrance doors and went away. Only the man in gray remained behind the glass wall. It was almost dark outside.

Jensen stepped into one of the aluminum-lined elevators and pressed the top button on the panel. The elevator stopped with a swift, sucking motion at the eighteenth floor, the doors opened and closed, then it started again.

The corridors in the comic strip editorial department were still and brightly lit, but the sounds behind the doors had ceased. He stood still and listened and after about thirty seconds, he heard an elevator stop somewhere in the vicinity, presumably one floor below. He waited for a while longer but heard no footsteps. He could hear nothing whatsoever, but all the same the silence was not absolute Not until he leaned to one side and pressed his ear to the concrete wall, could he make out the pulsating rumble from the far distant machine-rooms. When he had listened long enough, the sound grew more palpable, tormenting and demanding, like some unidentified pain.

He straightened up and went along the corridor. All the time he was conscious of the sound. Where the staircase ceased there were two white steel doors, one slightly larger than the other. Both were handleless. He took out the key with the strangely shaped head and tried it first in the smaller door, but it did not fit. The other one opened at once though, and he saw a steep narrow concrete stairway, dimly lit by small white bulbs.

Jensen went up the stairs, opened another door and came out on the roof.

It was quite dark and the evening wind was cold and biting. Around the flat roof ran a low parapet about three feet high. Far below lay the city with millions and yet more millions of cold white points of light. In the middle of the roof stood about ten low chimneys. Smoke was coming out of two of them and despite the wind he could smell the fumes, acrid, heavy, and suffocating.

He opened the upper door of the stairway and thought he heard someone shutting the lower one, but when he got down, the thirtieth floor seemed empty, silent and abandoned. He tried the master-key in the lock of the smaller door again but still could not open it. Presumably the door led to the machinery.

Once again he walked around the enclosed corridor, out of habit silently and cautiously in his rubber-soled shoes. On the far short side he stopped and listened again and thought he could make out footsteps somewhere in the vicinity. The sounds ceased immediately. It could have been an echo.

He took out the master-key again, opened a door and went into one of the editorial offices. It was slightly bigger than one of the cells in the Sixteenth Division's basement, the concrete walls bare and white, the ceiling too, and the floor light gray. The furniture consisted of three white tables which practically covered the floor surface and on the window-sill stood a chromium inter-office telephone. On the table lay paper, drawings, rulers and pens, all very tidily.

Jensen stopped beside one of them and looked at the colored drawing, which was divided into four squares and was evidently part of a comic strip. To one side of the illustration lay a page of typescript with the heading: "Original manuscript from author's department."

The first drawing was of a scene in a restaurant. A

blonde woman with enormous breasts and a glittering low cut dress was sitting at a table opposite a man wearing a blue mask over his eyes and dressed in tights with a broad leather belt. On the middle of his chest was a skull. In the background could be seen a dance orchestra and people in evening dress, and on the table was a bottle of champagne with two glasses. On the next there was only the man in the strange costume, a halo around his head and his right hand thrust into something like a primus stove. The next square showed the restaurant again; now the man in tights was up in the air above the table, while the blonde looked expressionlessly at him. The last illustration showed the man in tights, still in the air, and in the background were stars. From a ring on his right forefinger grew a gigantic hand on a long handle. In the hand lay an orange.

On the pictures were patches covered with white paint, some along the top edge, some in ovals leading to the shining teeth of the figures. These were filled with short, easily read texts, printed with Indian ink, but still incomplete.

"That evening Blue Panther meets the rich Beatrice at New York's smartest restaurant.
"I think . . . it feels so strange . . . I think that I . . . love you."
"What? I thought the moon moved!"
Blue Panther creeps out and loads his power-ring.
"Sorry, but I must leave you for a while. There's something wrong with the moon."
And once again Blue Panther leaves the woman he loves to save the world from certain destruction. It is the devilish Krysmopompas who"

He recognized the figures from one of the magazines he had studied the day before.

Fastened to the wall above the table was a stencilled notice. He read:

"During the last quarter our circulation has increased by 26%. The paper is satisfying a vital need and has a great task ahead. The bridgehead has been captured. Now we are fighting on toward final victory! Editor.

Jensen gave a last look at the illustrations, switched off the light and clicked the door behind him.

He rode down and found himself in the offices of one of the larger magazines. He now, distinctly and regularly, heard the slight sounds from whoever was following him. So that was settled and he need not bother about it any more.

He opened two doors and went into exactly identical concrete cells to those he had seen on the thirtieth floor. On the tables lay pictures of royalty, idols, children, dogs and cats, as well as articles which were being translated or rewritten. Some of them had been worked over with a red pen.

He read through a few and found that what had been struck out were almost without exception modestly critical observations and judgments of different kinds. The articles were on foreign pop stars.

The editor's room was larger than the others. The floor was covered with a light beige carpet and the tubular furniture had white braid upholstery. On the desk, apart from the loudspeaker-apparatus, lay two white telephones, a light gray blotter and a photograph in a steel frame. The photograph was clearly of the editor himself, a thin, middle-aged man with a troubled look, dog eyes and a well-clipped moustache.

Jensen sat down at the desk. When he cleared his throat, it echoed in the room, which seemed cold and desolate and larger than it was in reality. There were no books or papers in it, but on the white wall immediately opposite the desk hung a large framed color photograph. The picture had been taken at night and was of the building floodlit.

He opened a few drawers but found nothing of interest. In one of them lay a taped brown envelope on which was written Private. It contained some color photographs and a printed slip which read: *This is an exclusive offer at discount price from the Company's international picture service, reserved for heads of departments.* The photographs were of naked women with big pink breasts and shaved private parts.

Jensen resealed the envelope and put it back in its place. There was no law against such pictures, but after a sudden rage for them a few years back, the production of pornography had for some reason vanished from the market. In some quarters, the lack of demand was associated with the rapidly falling birth-rate.

He lifted the blotter and found an inter-office directive from the managing director.

> *The reporting on the wedding at the Royal Palace between the Princess and the Chairman of the Provincial Organization is objectionable. Several important people closely connected with the Company are hardly mentioned. The allusion to the bridegroom's brother having been an enthusiastic republican in his youth is outrageous, as is also the "humorous" thrust about the possibility of the*

Chairman of the Provincial Organization becoming king. Otherwise, as a journalist, I dislike the report's clumsy style. The letter in no. 8 should not, of course, have been included.

The statement that the suicide-rate in our country has fallen could lead to the disturbing misapprehension that far too many suicides took place earlier in our socially egalitarian society. Need I point out that the figures for your magazine are not rising according to the Company's estimates?

According to a note in the margin, copies of this directive had gone out to all heads of departments.

When Jensen came out into the corridor again, he thought he heard a slight rustling sound through one of the closed doors.

He took out the master-key, opened the door and went in. The light was out in the room, but in the reflection from the floodlights he saw a man hunched up in a chair. He shut the door behind him and switched on the light. The room was ordinary, with concrete walls and chromium window frames. The air was heavy and suffocating, smelling of liquor, cigarette smoke and vomit.

The man in the chair looked about fifty. He was large, rather fat, and was wearing a jacket, a white shirt, tie, shoes and socks. His trousers lay spread on the table and he had obviously been trying to clean them, and his long underwear was hanging on the radiator. His chin was resting on his chest and his face was flushed. On the table stood a plastic mug and an empty bottle of spirits, and between his feet a light metal waste-paper basket.

The man blinked in the sharp light and stared with bloodshot eyes.

"Journalism is dead," he said. "I am dead. Everything is dead."

He fumbled for the bottle on the table.

"Here I sit... in this damn soup-kitchen. Ordered about and treated like a dog by illiterates. Me! Year after year."

He had seized the bottle and poured out the last drop.

"The biggest damn soup-kitchen in the world," he said. "Three hundred and fifty thousand helpings a week. Lie-soup, guaranteed tasteless. Year after year."

His body shook all over and he had to use both hands to bring the mug to his lips.

"But now it's the end," he said.

He picked up a letter from the table and waved it about.

"Read that," he said. "Look at the finale."

Jensen took the paper. It was a message from the editor.

"Your reporting on the wedding at the Palace lacks discrimination, is badly written and full of inaccuracies. The publication of the letter in no. 8 is a scandalous lapse. I had to report the matter to the highest authority."

"He had of course read it all before it was set. The damn letter too. But I won't say anything about it. The poor son of a bitch is only saving his own skin."

The man looked at Jensen with renewed interest.

"Who are you? Some new director? You'll like it here, boy. There are dolled-up farm boys here, from some stinking muckheap in the country, all editors. And of course, old village bumpkins someone's made a bosh with."

Jensen took out his blue card. The man in the chair did not look at it. He said:

"I've been a journalist for thirty years. I've watched the spiritual decay. The intellectual strangulation. The slowest garrotting in the world. Before, I wanted something.

That was wrong. I still want a little, only a little. That's wrong too. I can write. That's wrong. So they hate me. But they've still got to have some like me. Until someone invents a machine with levers and buttons that'll write their damn lies, six pages an hour, without faults, erasures or ideas. Now I'm drunk. Hurrah, hurrah, hurrah."

His eyes were wide open and the pupils very small.

"And that poor silly bastard just hangs there like a boiled macaroon," he said.

He made a vague gesture toward his sex organ, hunched up again and mumbled:

"As soon as my trousers are dry, I'll try to get myself home."

The man sat in silence for a moment. He was breathing unevenly and heavily. Then he flung out his right arm and said:

"Highly honored public! Our play is done, our hero hanged, for human kind changes not and gives nothing without toll. Do you know who wrote that?"

"No," said Chief Inspector Jensen.

He turned out the light and left the room.

On the tenth floor, he changed to the service elevator and went down in it all the way to the paper store.

The night lights were on, occasional blue bulbs which spread a weak and uncertain glow.

He stood quite still and felt the pressure from the huge building above him. The rotary presses and the machines were still and the massiveness and weight of the building seemed to add to the silence. He could no longer hear the sounds of whoever had been following him.

He rode up to street level. The vestibule was empty and he waited. Three minutes elapsed before the man in the gray suit came out from a side door and walked toward the attendant's cubby-hole.

"There's a drunk in room two thousand one hundred forty-three," said Jensen.

"He's been seen to," said the man in gray tonelessly.

Jensen opened the door with his own key and went out into the cold air.

When he got back to the Sixteenth Division station, it was five to ten. There was nothing of interest in his office, so he went down to the cell floor, where two young women were being hustled through the doors. He waited while they handed over their identity cards, shoes, coats, and handbags at the control counter. One of them swore and spat at the man on duty. The constable who made the arrests yawned and twisted her wrist as he glanced wearily at his watch. The other girl stood still, her head down and her arms hanging loosely. She was crying and mumbled as she sniffed. The words were the same old ones, "no, no," and "I don't want to."

The girls were hustled away by two policewomen in rubber boots and pale green plastic overalls and soon afterward came the whimpers and cries from the physical examination. The women staff were both more effective and more tenacious than the men.

He went over to the control counter and read down the list of those who had been booked during the last hour or two. No one had been arrested at the company and no report had come in from there.

Jensen ate nothing on the way home. He was not

especially hungry and he could no longer feel the churning in his stomach. But despite the warmth and security of the car, he was trembling as if with cold, and he found it difficult to keep his hands still on the wheel.

He undressed at once and went straight to bed. After lying in the darkness for an hour, he arose and got the bottle. The trembling stopped after a while, but he was still cold when he fell asleep.

The third day had gone. He had four left.

12

The morning was clear and cold. A thin layer of newly fallen snow covered the grass between the blocks of apartments, and films of surface ice lay on the concrete of the highway.

Jensen had woken early and in spite of the lines of cars and the slippery roads, he was in his office in good time. His throat was dry and although he had both gargled and brushed his teeth, the stale, musty taste still lay on his tongue. He sent out for a bottle of mineral water from the canteen and began to go through the papers on his desk. The report from the Criminal Technical Institute had not arrived and the others contained nothing of interest. The man at the post office had come to a full stop. Jensen read carefully through his laconic report, massaged his temples with the tips of his fingers and dialed the number of the main post office. A long time elapsed before the policeman came to the telephone.

"Jensen here."

"Yes, sir."

"What are you doing?"

"Questioning the sorters. It'll take a long time."

"Be specific."

"Two more days. Perhaps three."

"Do you think it'll lead anywhere?"

"Doubt it. There are lots of letters addressed with cutout newspaper headlines. I've already seen over a hundred. Most aren't even anonymous. People do it all the same."

"Why?"

"Some sort of joke, I suppose. The only person who remembers this particular letter is the messenger who delivered it."

"Have you a copy of the letter itself?"

"No, sir. But I've got one of the envelope and the address."

"I know. Avoid superfluous information."

"Yes, sir."

"Stop searching. Go to the Criminal Technical laboratory, have a photostat copy made of the text and find out from which newspaper or newspapers the letters were gotten. Right?"

"Right, sir."

Jensen replaced the receiver. Outside the window, the sanitation squad was rattling about with shovels and metal cans.

He clasped his hands together and waited.

When he had waited for three hours and twenty minutes, the telephone rang.

"We've identified the paper," said the laboratory man.

"Yes?"

"A document paper, quality CB-3. Manufactured in one of the concern's own paper factories."

Silence fell for a moment. Then the man said:

"Not all that remarkable in itself. They own practically the whole of the paper industry."

"Stick to the point," said Jensen.

"This factory is up north, only about thirty miles from the city. We've a man up there now. I talked to him about five minutes ago."

"And?"

"The type has been in use about a year. It's mostly reserved for export, but small quantities have been sent directly to so-called civil printing firms, which also belong to the concern. It's been delivered there in two different cuts. As far as I can make out, this is a question of the larger format only. We won't follow the matter up any further. The rest is your business. I've sent a messenger with all the information on addresses and names. You should have them in about ten minutes."

Jensen did not reply.

"That's all," said the laboratory man.

The man seemed to hesitate. After a brief uncertain pause, he said:

"Inspector Jensen?"

"Yes."

"That matter yesterday . . . I mean, the report for dereliction of duty. Does that still stand?"

"Certainly," said Jensen.

Ten minutes later a man brought the written information.

When Jensen had finished reading, he rose and looked at the large map on the wall. Then he put on his coat and went down to his car.

13

The office had glass walls and while Jensen was waiting for the manager of the printing firm to return, he watched the activities on the other side, where the staff in white and gray coats moved to and fro behind long benches. In the background he heard the clatter of the type-setting machines and presses.

Still wet proof-sheets hung on steel hooks along one wall of the office. The texts, set with large thick type, lauded the company's newspapers. One of them stated that a certain newspaper that week was bringing out a life-size panoramic supplement of a sixteen-year-old television star. The supplement was produced in "lovely multi-colored print of rare beauty." The public was exhorted to buy the paper at once before the edition was sold out.

"We do some of the company's advertising," said the manager. "Those are ads for daily papers. Handsome but expensive. One of those costs five times as much as you or I earn in a year."

Jensen said nothing.

"But that obviously doesn't matter much to the owner of the whole lot, the weeklies, the dailies, the printing firms and the paper they print on," said the manager.

"But they're a fine job all the same," he said.

The man turned away and put a throat pastille in his mouth.

"You were quite right," he said. "We've printed two things on that paper. About a year ago. Damned good jobs they were too. Not large quantities. Just a few thousand each. One a private letter-head for the Chief, the other some kind of diploma."

"For the company?"

"Yes, of course. There should be some trial pulls here somewhere. You can see for yourself."

He hunted among his files.

"Yes, here they are."

The Chief's notepaper was quite small with an elegant heading, and the discreet gray cipher in the upper right hand corner seemed to be deliberately demonstrating modest and sober taste. Jensen saw at once that the paper was considerably smaller than the anonymous letter, but he measured it all the same. Then he took out the report from the laboratory and compared the two. The figures did not agree.

The other article was an almost square four-sided folder. The first two sides were blank, but on the third was a text printed in gold in large elaborate Gothic lettering. It ran:

WE EXPRESS OUR HEARTFELT GRATITUDE FOR THE PAST YEARS' BENEFICIAL CO-OPERATION IN THE SERVICE OF CULTURE AND SOCIAL EQUALITY.

"Damned fine job, that, isn't it?"

"What is it for?"

"No idea. Some sort of diploma. Someone signs them, I

suppose. Then it's presented, I suppose. I expect that's the idea."

Jensen took a ruler and measured the front of the folder. He took out the piece of paper from his pocket and compared the measurements. They agreed.

"Have you got this type of paper in stock?"

"No, it's a special job. Very expensive too. And what was left over when we did the job is bound to have been pulped long ago."

"I'll take this with me."

"We've only got this one for the records," said the manager.

"Oh yes," said Jensen.

The manager was a man of sixty with a lined face and melancholy eyes. He smelt of drink, printing ink and throat lozenges, and he said nothing else, not even good-bye.

Jensen rolled up the diploma and left.

14

The personnel manager's room was on the nineteenth floor. The man at the desk was a thick-set fat man with a frog face and his smile was not quite so practised as the managing director's. It just looked crooked, twisted, and malicious. He said:

"Deaths? Yes, naturally there've been a few jumps."

"Jumps?"

"Yes. Suicides. They occur . . . here and there."

His observation was correct. During the past year, two pedestrians in the center of the city had been killed by falling bodies. Several others had been injured. This was one of the disadvantages of building high.

"And otherwise?"

"A few people have died in the building lately, I suppose, always of natural causes or accidents. I'll get a secretary to send over a list."

"Thank you."

. The personnel manager made a strenuous effort. He succeeded in improving on his smile a little and said:

"Can I be of any further assistance to you?"

"Yes," said Jensen, unrolling the diploma. "What is this?"

The man looked slightly put out.

"An address, or perhaps I should say a testimonial, to those who leave our employ. It is very expensively produced, to give our employees a beautiful souvenir. Then no expense is spared. That's what the company directors think, in this case as in so many other things."

"This is presented to everyone who leaves here?"

The man shook his head.

"No, no, of course not. That would be much too costly. This is a token of honor which is usually only presented to people in leading positions or to especially trusted colleagues. Under any circumstances, those who receive it must have done their duty and acted as worthy ambassadors of the company."

"How many have been presented?"

"Only a few. This particular type is quite new. We haven't used it for more than six months."

"Where are the diplomas kept?"

"My secretary keeps them."

"Are they easily accessible?"

The personnel manager pressed a button on the intercom. A young woman came into the room.

"Is form PR-8 easily accessible to outsiders?"

The woman looked frightened.

"No, certainly not. They're in the big steel cupboard. I lock it every time I leave the room."

He waved her out and said:

"The girl's reliable and very thorough. Otherwise she wouldn't be here."

"I need a list of the people who have received diplomas of this kind."

"Of course. That can be arranged."

They sat in silence for a long while as they waited for the list to be made out. Finally Jensen said:

"What are your main duties?"

"To appoint office and administrative staff. To see to it that everything is done for the personnel's welfare, and . . ."

He paused briefly and smiled a broad smile with his frog mouth. It was hard and cold and looked absolutely genuine.

"And to rid the company of those who abuse our trust," he said, "and deal with those who misbehave."

After a second or two, he added:

"Yes, yes, it happens in extreme cases of necessity and in the most humane way, like everything else here."

Silence again fell in the room. Jensen sat without moving, listening to the pulsating rhythm of the building.

The secretary came in with two copies of a list. It consisted of twelve names.

The personnel manager read it.

"Two of these people have died since they were retired," he said. "And one has to my certain knowledge gone to live abroad."

He took out his fountain pen and put neat little ticks against three of the names. Then he handed the paper to his visitor.

Jensen glanced quickly down the list. After each name stood date of birth and a few bits of information, for instance, "retired early" or "retired at own request." Carefully he folded the piece of paper and put it in his pocket.

Before he left, a few more remarks were exchanged.

"May I ask what occasions your interest in this particular detail?"

"A duty which I have no authority to discuss."

"Has one of our testimonials fallen into the wrong hands?"

"I don't think so."

There were already two men in the elevator Jensen went down in. They were quite young and were smoking cigarettes as they talked about the weather. Their jargon was nervous and staccato and seemed to consist of a series of key words. It was not easy for an outsider to understand.

When the elevator stopped at the eighteenth floor, the Chief stepped in. He nodded absently and stood with his face to the wall. Both the journalists put out their cigarettes and took off their hats.

"Fancy snowing," said one in a low voice.

"I'm sorry for the poor little flowers," said the Chief, in his fine deep voice.

He said this without glancing at the young man who had spoken. He stood without moving, his face turned to the aluminum wall. Nothing more was said on the way down.

In the vestibule, Jensen borrowed a telephone and called the laboratory.

"Well?"

"You were right. There are traces of gold-dust. In the glue under the letters. Odd that we overlooked it."

"Do you think so?"

15

"Find this person's address. It's urgent."

The head of the Civil Patrol jerked to attention and left.

Jensen studied the note that lay on the desk before him. He opened one of the drawers, took out a ruler and drew thin straight lines through three of the names. Then he numbered the remainder from one to nine, looked at the time and made a neat note at the top of the piece of paper: Thursday. 4.25 p.m.

He took out an unused notebook, turned to the first page and wrote: Number 1. Ex-distribution manager, 48 years old, married, retired early because of ill-health.

Two minutes later the head of the Civil Patrol came back with the address. Jensen wrote it down, closed the notebook and rose.

"Get information on the others," he said. "It must be done by the time I get back."

He drove through the city's office and shopping center, past the Trade Union Palace and followed the stream of west-bound traffic. The lines of cars moved rapidly along the wide straight highway, which cut through the industrial district and the scattered dormitory towns with their thousands of tall blocks of apartments lined up in identical columns.

In the clear light of the evening sun, he could see the layer of exhaust fumes quite clearly. It was about forty feet thick and lay like a poisonous bank of fog over the city.

An hour or two earlier, he had drunk two cups of tea and eaten four biscuits. Now he had a pain on the right side of his diaphragm, heavy and grinding, like a drill rotating slowly in the soft tissues of his body. In spite of the pain, he was still hungry.

After a few miles, the blocks of apartments began to grow older and more decayed. They rose like pillars out of the unkempt overgrown vegetation, large patches of the facing fallen away from the uneven concrete blocks and many windows broken. Since the authorities had succeeded in overcoming the housing shortage ten years earlier by the building of a series of high blocks of identical standard apartments, many of the older residential districts had become depopulated. In several such suburbs, scarcely a third of the apartments were now occupied. The rest stood empty and were falling into disrepair. The blocks were no longer rentable and no one bothered to repair and maintain them. They had also been poorly constructed and rapidly fell into decay. Many of the shops had gone bankrupt and closed down, or had simply been abandoned by their owners. Since the government thought that every person should have a car of his own, there was no longer any local or state transportation running in these areas.

In the bushy undergrowth around the buildings lay heaps of abandoned cars and indestructible plastic contain-ers. The Ministry of the Interior reckoned that the buildings gradually would be completely abandoned and then collapse, thus transforming the areas automatically, and at no extra cost, into rubbish dumps.

He turned off the highway, drove across the bridge and found himself on a long island with trees, swimming pools, tennis courts, bridle paths and white houses along the shore. After a few minutes he slowed down, swung to the left, drove between some tall wrought-iron gates, up to a house and stopped.

The house was large and expensive and gave an impression of luxury with its well-polished glass façade. To one side of the front door stood three cars, of which one was large and silver-gray, the latest model of a foreign make.

Jensen went up the steps and as he passed the photo-electric cell, he heard the sound of chiming bells from inside the house. The door was opened by a young woman in a black dress and a starched white lace cap. She asked him to wait and vanished into the house. The interior of the hall and what he could see of the house was modernistic and impersonal. It had the same chilly elegance as the directors' department in the company building.

There was also a youngster of about nineteen in the hall. He was sitting in one of the tubular armchairs with his legs stretched out in front of him and was staring apathetically ahead.

The man Jensen had come to see was a sunburnt, blue-eyed man with a bull neck, the beginnings of a paunch and a supercilious expression. He was dressed in slacks, sandals, and a short smart smoking jacket made of some fluffy material.

"What's it about?" he snapped. "I must tell you here and now that I've very little time indeed."

Jensen took a step into the hall and showed his badge.

"The name's Jensen," he said. "Chief Inspector Jensen from the Sixteenth Division. I'm carrying out an investigation which concerns your former post and place of employment."

The man's stance and facial expression altered. He shifted his feet uneasily and seemed to collapse inwardly. His eyes became frightened and restless.

"For God's sake," he mumbled. "Not here, in front of . . . Come into my . . . or the library . . . Yes, the library would be better."

He gestured uncertainly, apparently searching for some diversion and said:

"This is my son."

The young man in the armchair gave them a bored glance.

"Wouldn't you like to go for a drive and try out your new car?" said the man in the smoking jacket.

"What for?"

"Well, girls and . . ."

"Ugh!" said the youngster.

His eyes clouded over again.

"I don't understand the young nowadays," the man said with a bewildered smile.

Jensen did not reply and the smile at once died away.

There were no books in the library, which was a large light room containing a few cupboards and several low sets of chairs. On the table lay magazines.

The man in the smoking jacket carefully shut the doors

and threw an appealing look at his visitor, whose face was rigid and serious. Then he shuddered and went over to one of the cupboards, took out a glass, practically filled it with liquor and drank the contents in one draught. Then he poured out another, looked at Jensen again and mumbled:

"Well, it doesn't matter now, I suppose. You wouldn't like some yourself . . . no, of course not . . . sorry . . . You understand perhaps, the shock . . ."

The man collapsed into one of the chairs. Jensen remained standing. The other man's face was already glistening with sweat. He kept wiping his face with a folded handkerchief.

"Oh, my God," he said. "I knew it. I've known it all along. That those damn swines would stick a knife into me as soon as the election was over."

"But I'll make a stand," he said aggressively. "They'll take everything I've got, of course. But I know a thing or two, I know one or two things, things they don't . . ."

Jensen looked at him steadily.

"There are one or two things," said the man. "There are figures which they'd find very hard to explain away. Do you know what their taxes amount to? Do you know where their tax lawyers are *really* employed?"

He pushed his fingers nervously through his thinning hair and said unhappily:

"Yes, yes, forgive me . . . Of course, I don't mean to . . . my position could hardly be worse, but . . ."

Suddenly his voice grew earnest.

"Must you question me here though, in my own home? I suppose you know everything. Must you stand like that? Why don't you sit down?"

Jensen remained standing. He still said nothing. The man emptied his glass and put it down with a bang. His hands were shaking.

"Yes, yes, get going then," he said. "Let's get it over and done with. So we can get away from here."

He rose and went back to the cupboard, fumbling with the glass and cap of the bottle.

Jensen opened his notebook and took out his pen.

"When did you leave your job?" he said.

"Last autumn. The tenth of September. I'll never forget that day. Nor the weeks before it either. They were terrible, just as terrible as this day, today."

"You were retired early?"

"Of course. They forced me to. Out of sheer goodwill, naturally. I even got a doctor's certificate. They'd thought of everything. Heart trouble, they said. Heart trouble sounds good. I was, of course, completely fit."

"And the amount of your pension?"

"I was given full salary and have been receiving it ever since. Good God, it was chicken feed compared with what they have to pay their tax consultants. And they could stop paying me when they felt like it. I signed the papers."

"What papers?"

"The statement, as they called it. The confession. You've read it, I suppose? And the conveyance of the house here and my means. They only wanted it *pro forma,* they said, not to use it, unless it proved absolutely necessary. Well, I've never had any illusions about it. I just thought it wouldn't prove necessary so soon. For a long time I've been trying to persuade myself they wouldn't report me, that they'd never dare face the scandal of a public trial and all the talk. They had me on the hook anyhow—this"—he made a sweeping gesture—"is compensation for their loss I suppose, even if the sum seemed large."

"How large?"

"Over half a million. Look, must I repeat it all over again? Verbally . . . and here . . . at home?"

"Was it all in cash?"

"No, not quite half of it. And it was spread over many years. The rest . . ."

"Yes?"

"The rest was materials, building materials mostly, transport, labor, paper, envelopes. That bastard had it all down, even the paper-clips, the rubber bands and the glue, I think."

"Who?"

"That bastard who did the investigation. Their favorite dog, the managing director. I never saw them once. They didn't want to soil their hands with such things, he said. And no one found out a thing. It would do the firm irretrievable harm, he said. There was an election shortly afterward. I thought perhaps they'd just wait until it was over."

He kept mopping his face with his handkerchief, which was already gray and soaking wet.

"What . . . what are you going to do with me?"

"When you stopped working there, did you receive some kind of diploma, a testimonial?"

The man in the smoking jacket shuddered.

"Yes," he said tonelessly.

"Please show it to me."

"Now?"

"Yes, at once."

The man rose unsteadily, tried to adjust his expression and went out of the room. A few minutes later he returned with the diploma. It was covered with a piece of glass and in a broad gold frame. The text was signed by the Chief and the publisher.

"There was a page with no printing on it. What have you done with it?"

The man looked at Jensen in confusion.

"Don't know. Threw it away, I suppose. I think I cut it off before I took it to the framer's."

"You don't remember for certain?"

"No. I must have thrown it away afterward. I remember cutting it off."

"With scissors?"

"Yes, yes, that I'm certain of."

He stared at the picture and shook it.

"What a fraud," he mumbled. "What hypocrisy, what a bloody fraud."

"Yes," said Jensen.

He closed his notebook, put it in his pocket and rose to his feet.

"Good-bye," he said.

The man looked at him uncomprehendingly.

"When . . . when are you coming back?"

"Don't know," said Jensen.

The youth in the hall was still sitting in the same position, but now he was studying his horoscope in a magazine with a slight glimmer of interest.

It was already dark when Jensen drove back, and in the decayed dormitory towns, the tall blocks stood like lines of black ghosts in the undergrowth.

He did not bother to go to his office, but drove straight home. On the way, he stopped at a cafeteria. Although he was perfectly aware of the consequences, he ate three sandwiches and drank two mugs of black coffee.

The fourth day had gone.

16

When the telephone rang, Jensen had not yet had time to get dressed. It was five to seven in the morning and he was standing in front of the bathroom mirror, shaving. During the night he had had a severe attack of colic, now the pain had eased but his diaphragm still felt tender and mangled.

He knew it had something to do with the job, for he never used the telephone for private calls and did not allow anyone else to do so either.

"Jensen," said the Chief of Police, "what the hell are you up to?"

"We've still three days at our disposal."

"I didn't mean that."

"I've hardly had time to begin the interrogations."

"I didn't mean the tempo, Jensen."

There was no answer to that. The Chief of Police coughed raucously.

"Fortunately for you and for me, the matter's settled."

"Settled?"

"Yes, they've found the culprit themselves."

"Who have?"

"The concern's own staff. As we thought in the beginning, it was a joke that misfired. One of their employees, a journalist on one of the papers. Evidently a rather bohemian young man with a lot of wild ideas, but all right underneath. They seemed to have suspected him from the start, but didn't bother to say so."

"I see."

"I suppose they didn't want to bring up any unfounded suspicions.

"I see."

"Anyhow, the whole thing's settled. They're not bringing a charge against him. All you need do is collect his confession. Then you can close the case."

"I see."

"I have the man's name and address here. Got a pen?"

Jensen wrote down the information on the back of a little white card.

"It would be best for all concerned if you go there as quickly as possible. So that we're done with the case."

"Yes."

"Complete the case then in the usual way and transcribe it. In the event they want to know about the investigation."

"I see."

"Jensen?"

"Yes."

"You've no reason to be despondent. It's quite reasonable that it happened this way. Naturally the concern's own people had greater opportunities to clear the matter up. Their knowledge of the personnel and the internal circumstances gave them a great advantage."

Jensen said nothing. The Chief of Police was breathing heavily and unevenly.

"There's something else too," he said.

"Yes."

"I indicated from the start that you should devote your attentions to the threatening letter, didn't I?"

"Yes, that's correct."

"That also means that you neither need nor should take any notice of any other circumstances that may arise during the investigation. When this young joker's confession has been verified, you can put the case to one side. Then you can forget it all. Right?"

"Right."

"I think it'd be best for all concerned . . as I said, not least for me and you."

"I see."

"Good. Good-bye."

Jensen went back to the bathroom and completed his shave. Then he dressed, drank a cup of honey-water and read the morning paper, all without haste.

Although the traffic was less thick than usual, he kept to a moderate speed on the highway and when he parked outside the station, it was already half-past nine.

He sat at his desk for a while without looking at the reports or the list of addresses. Then he called for the man in the Civil Patrol, gave him the white card and said:

"Get hold of some information on this person. Everything you can find. It's urgent."

He stood by the window for a long time, watching the sanitation squad, who had not yet had time to finish the disinfecting when two policemen in green uniforms brought in the day's first drunks. After a while, the man who had formerly been at the post office called.

"Where are you?"

"At the central newspaper records."

"Any results?"

"Not yet. Shall I go on?"

"Yes," said Jensen.

The head of the Civil Patrol came back about an hour later.

"Well?"

"Twenty-six years old. Son of well-known businessman. Family considered wealthy. Works as a journalist on weekly papers. Good education. Unmarried. Considered favored by the bosses, thanks to family connections, I should think. Character . . ."

The policeman frowned and studied the piece of paper as if he were finding it difficult to read his own handwriting.

"Unstable, spontaneous, charming, humorous. Given to drastic practical jokes. Bad nerves, not very reliable, soon tires. Seven times drunk, two periods at alcoholic clinics.

"Sounds like a bad lot," said the head of the Civil Patrol.

"It's enough," said Jensen.

At half-past twelve, he had his lunch brought up from the canteen, two lightly boiled eggs, a mug of tea and three biscuits.

When he had finished eating he rose, put on his hat and coat, went down to his car and drove south.

He found the address, two floors up in an ordinary block, but no one answered the door when he rang. He listened and thought he could hear faint sounds of music inside the apartment. After a minute or two, he tried the handle. The door was unlocked and he went in.

The apartment was a standard one with a hall, kitchen and two rooms. The walls of the first room were bare and there were no curtains. In the middle of the floor stood a wooden chair and beside it an empty brandy bottle. On the chair sat a naked man playing a guitar.

He put his head on one side and looked at the visitor, but neither stopped playing nor said anything.

Jensen went on into the other room. It had neither furniture nor carpets, nor curtains, but on the floor lay several bottles and a heap of clothes. On a mattress in one corner, a woman lay asleep, wrapped up in sheets and blankets and with her head buried in the pillow. One arm was resting on the floor and within reach she had cigarettes, a brown braid bag and an ashtray.

The atmosphere was thick and musty with liquor, cigarette smoke and naked human bodies. Jensen opened the window.

The woman raised her head from the pillow and stared at him uncomprehendingly.

"Who the hell are you?" she said. "What are you doing here?"

"It's the detective we've been waiting for all day, darling," called the guitar-player from the next room. "The great detective who has come to expose us."

"Go to hell," said the woman and let her head fall back on the pillow.

Jensen went across to the mattress.

"Show your identity card," he said.

"Go to hell," she said, thickly and sleepily.

He bent down, opened her bag and found the card after a brief search. He eyed through the personal details. She was nineteen years old. On the upper right hand border were two red marks, quite visible although someone had tried to rub them out. They meant two charges of drunkenness. A third would involve immediate removal to an alcoholic-clinic.

Jensen left the apartment. At the door, he stopped and turned to the guitar-player.

"I'll be back in five minutes. You must be dressed by then."

He went down to the car and called a police bus. It came within three minutes and he took two constables up with him to the apartment. The guitar-player had put on his shirt and trousers and was sitting smoking on the window-sill. The woman was still asleep.

One of the constables took out an alcohol-tester, lifted the woman's head up and thrust the mouthpiece between her lips.

"Breathe out," he said.

The crystals in the plastic bladder turned green.

"Get dressed," said the policeman.

The woman woke up at once. She leapt out of the bedclothes, clutching a sheet to her breasts, her hands trembling.

"No," she said. "No, you can't. I haven't done anything. I live here. You can't. No, no, for God's sake, no."

"Get dressed," said the constable with the alcohol-tester, pushing her clothes toward her with his foot.

"No, I don't want to," she cried, flinging the clothes across the floor.

"Take her in the blanket," said Jensen. "I'm in a hurry."

She stared at him, wildly and dumbly, fear in her eyes.

The right side of her face was marked with red streaks from the pillow, her short dark hair rumpled and untidy.

Jensen went into the other room. The man was still sitting by the window. The woman cried, shrilly and hysterically and seemed to be offering some resistance, but it did not last for very long. In less than two minutes, the policemen had overpowered her and taken her away. Jensen noted the time by his watch.

"Was that really necessary?" said the man in the window.

His voice was cultivated but uncertain, and his hands were trembling.

"So it was you who sent the letter?" said Jensen.

"Yes. I confess. I've already done so once."

"When did you mail it?"

"On Sunday."

"What time?"

"In the evening. I don't remember what time."

"Before or after nine o'clock?"

"After, I think. I've told you, I can't remember what time."

"Where did you make up the letter?"

"At home."

"Here?"

"No, at my parents' home."

"What sort of paper did you use?"

"An ordinary bit of white paper."

He was gaining confidence and was looking coldly at Jensen.

"Typing paper?"

"No, better quality. A bit of some kind of diploma."

"Where did you get it from?"

"At the company. It was lying about there. People who leave or get the sack usually get diplomas like that. Shall I describe it?"

"No need. Where did you find it?"

"At the company, I told you."

"Be specific."

"It was just lying about. Someone had it to see what it was like, or something like that."

"Did you find it on a table?"

"I expect so."

He seemed to think.

"Perhaps it was on a shelf."

"When did this happen?"

"Oh, several months back. Believe it or not, but I really can't remember. No, in fact, I don't remember, but anyhow it wasn't this year."

"And you took it away with you then?"

"Yes."

"As a joke?"

"More to use it for some lark later on."

"Lark?"

"Joke. An old expression."

"What sort of joke?"

"Oh, you can use that sort of diploma for a lot of things. Sign false names on it and stick a naked bird on the front and send it to some idiot."

"When did you hit on the letter idea?"

"On Sunday. I had nothing special to do. So it occurred to me I might throw them into some confusion up there. It was only for fun. I didn't think they'd kick up such a fuss."

He was gaining more and more confidence and sharpness. Now he said appealingly:

"How was I to know there'd be such an almighty row? Never gave it a thought."

"What sort of glue did you use?"

"My own. Perfectly ordinary glue."

Jensen nodded.

"Show your identity card."

The man took out his card immediately. It had six red marks, all crossed out with blue.

"It's no good booking me for drunkenness. I've got three to go."

Jensen gave him back the card.

"She hadn't," the man said, nodding toward the other room. "Anyhow, it was virtually your fault. We'd been waiting for you since some time last night and what could we do? I can't bear sitting still. Poor kid."

"Is the woman your fiancée?"

"Yes, one could say that."

"Does she live here?"

"Yes, mostly. She's a good bird, but hard work. A little old-fashioned. A bit hot, if you get what I mean."

Jensen nodded.

"Look, what if the old man . . . if the lot up there hadn't been so kind as to withdraw the charge. What would I have got?"

"That would have been up to the court," said Jensen. He closed his notebook.

The man took out a cigarette and lit it. He had jumped down from the window-sill and was leaning in a relaxed way against the wall.

"God, the messes one gets into," he said. "Thank God I was born lucky."

Jensen put his notebook into his pocket and glanced at the door.

"Before you stuck the letters on, you tore the page in two, didn't you?"

"Yes, of course."

"You tore them apart?"

"Yes."

"You didn't cut them? With scissors?"

The man put his hand to the tip of his nose with a swift movement, stroked his eyebrows slowly, frowned, and then looked at Jensen.

"I'm not absolutely certain," he said at last.

"Try."

Pause.

"No, I can't remember."

"Where did you mail the letter?"

"Here in town."

"Be specific."

"In a mail box somewhere."

"Tell me exactly where the mail box is."

"I can't."

"Don't you know where you mailed the letter?"

"Yes, it was somewhere in town, I've said that. But exactly which mail box, I don't remember."

"No?"

"No, it'd be absurd if I remembered that. There are mail boxes all over the place, aren't there?"

Jensen did not reply.

"Aren't there?" said the man irritably.

"Yes, that's correct."

"Well, then."

"But you remember which part of the city you mailed it in?"

Jensen was looking expressionlessly out of the window. The other man tried to catch his eye. When he did not succeed, he turned away and said:

"No, I don't remember. Does it matter?"

"Where do your parents live?"

'Over on the east side."

"Perhaps you mailed the letter somewhere near where they live."

"I keep telling you. I don't know. What the hell does it matter?"

"Didn't you mail the letter here on the south side?"

"Oh hell, yes. No, I don't know."

"Where did you mail the letter?"

"I don't know," said the man hysterically.

He stopped, breathing heavily. After a brief pause, he said:

"I drove all around the city that night."

"Alone?"

"Yes."

"And you don't know where you mailed the letter?"

"No. How many times do I have to say so?"

He began to walk up and down the room with quick restless steps.

"So you don't remember?"

"No."

"You don't know where you mailed the letter?"

"No," screamed the young man uncontrollably.

"Get dressed and come with me," said Chief Inspector Jensen.

"Where to?"

"To the police station in the Sixteenth Division."

"Won't it do if I drop in and sign the papers tomorrow? I've . . . other things to do this evening."

"No."

"And if I refuse?"

"You've no right to refuse. You're under arrest."

"Arrest? What the hell do you mean, you damn flat-foot? They've withdrawn the charge, haven't they? What for?"

"For giving misleading information."

Not a word was spoken in the car. The young man sat in the back and Jensen could see him in the driving mirror almost without moving his eyes. The young man seemed nervous. He kept blinking behind his glasses and when he thought he was not being observed, he bit his nails.

Jensen drove into the yard and parked by the entrance. He took the young man past the control counter, on past the row of cells in which the drunks were either weeping or sitting hopelessly hunched up behind the shining steel bars, and he opened a door. The room inside was brightly lit. Ceiling, wall and floor were white and in the middle of the room stood a bakelite stool.

The young man looked around defiantly and irresolutely and then sat down on the stool. Jensen went away, turning the key in the door on the outside as he did so.

Up in his office, he picked up the telephone receiver, dialed three numbers and said:

"Send an interrogator down to isolation. A false confession which must be retracted. It's urgent."

Then he took a white card out of his breast pocket, put it down on the table and drew a very small five-pointed star in the top left-hand corner. Slowly and carefully he drew a row of similar stars across the width of the card. On the next row, he drew six-pointed stars, identical and very small. When he had filled in the bottom row, he counted the stars. Altogether he had drawn 1,242 stars, 633 five-pointed and 609 six-pointed ones.

He was irritated by the burning in his throat and the churning in his stomach, and drank a mug of bicarbonate. From the yard rose cries and other sounds of violent man-handling, but he did not bother to go to the window.

After four hours and twenty-five minutes, the telephone rang.

"All clear," said the interrogator. "It wasn't him, but he was hard to get at."

"And the statement?"

"Signed and sealed."

"The motive?"

"Money, I should think. Though he still refuses to admit it."

"Let him go."

"Will it go to court?"

"No."

"Easily done, now."

"No," said Jensen. "It's not necessary."

He put down the receiver, tore up the card covered with stars and threw the bits into the waste-paper basket. Then he picked up the list with the nine numbered names on it, turned to a new page in his notebook and wrote: Number 2. 42 years old, reporter, divorced, terminated employment at his own request.

Jensen drove home and went to bed without eating or drinking anything. He was very tired and the burning in his throat had gone, but it was a long time before he fell asleep.

This was the fifth day and it had been completely wasted.

17

"It was the wrong man," said Jensen.

"I don't understand it. What happened? He confessed, didn't he?"

"The confession had been dictated."

"And he admitted that?"

"Yes, later."

"You maintain then, that the man admitted to an offense he hadn't committed? Are you certain?"

"Yes."

"Are you clear about his reasons?"

"No."

"Won't that affect your investigations?"

"Not necessarily."

"Well, I suppose that's all to the good then," said the Chief of Police.

It sounded as if he were talking to himself.

"Jensen?"

"Yes."

"Your position at the moment is not an enviable one. As far as I know, the request to find the man still stands. You've just two days left. Will you make it?"

"I don't know."

"If you haven't laid hands on him by Monday I can't answer for the consequences. In fact I can't even anticipate them. Do I need to point this out?"

"No."

"Failure could also do me harm personally."

"I see."

"After this unexpected development, it is, of course, even more important that the investigation is carried out with the utmost discretion."

"I see."

"I am relying on your judgment. Good luck."

The Chief of Police had called at exactly the same time as on the previous morning, but Jensen was already on his way when the call came. He had had only two hours' sleep during the night but he felt fit all the same and fairly rested. The honey-water had, however, not quelled his hunger and the churning in his stomach showed no tendency to decline.

"I must eat some cooked food soon. Tomorrow, or at the latest the day after tomorrow."

He said this to himself as he walked down the stairs. It was very rare for him to talk to himself.

Light rain in the night had melted the covering of snow. The temperature was now just above the freezing point, the clouds had scattered and the sunlight was bright and cold.

At the Sixteenth Division station, the morning chores had not yet been completed. At the basement entrance stood the gray bus that was to take the third-time drunks to clinics and work-camps, and in the basement the staff were hustling sleepy disheveled people out of the cells. The policemen were haggard with fatigue and lack of sleep. Inside the door stood those who were to be released, waiting in a long silent line to pass the control and receive their injections.

Jensen stopped at the doctor's table.

"How was it last night?"

"Normal. That is, a bit worse than the night before."

Jensen nodded.

"We had a sudden death again last night. A woman."

"Oh yes."

"She even said so beforehand. That she had been drinking just to put an end to things and that the police had interrupted her. But I still couldn't stop her."

"What did she do?"

"Threw herself against the cell wall and cracked her skull. Quite difficult to do, but it apparently works."

The doctor looked at Jensen. His eyes were swollen and inflamed and there was a faint smell of liquor which did not seem to come from the man who had just had an injection.

"It takes both physical strength and a strong will," said the doctor. "And also one has to tear away the insulation."

Most of the people who had just been set free were standing about with their hands in their pockets and their heads bowed. There was neither fear nor despair in their faces, only emptiness.

Jensen went up to his office, took out one of his cards and made two notes.

Better wall insulation.

New doctor.

His office again had nothing of interest to offer and he left it almost immediately. It was twenty past eight.

18

The suburb was ten or so miles to the south and belonged to the category which in the Ministry was usually called "self-cleansing."

It had been built during the severe housing shortage and consisted of about thirty tall blocks of apartments, symmetrically arranged around a bus station and a so-called shopping center. Now the bus service had ceased and nearly all the shops were closed. The great paved piazza was used as a graveyard for cars and scarcely twenty percent of the apartments were occupied.

Jensen found the address after considerable trouble, parked his car and got out. The block had fourteen floors and on the places where the facing had not fallen away, the walls were black with damp. The paving stones in front of the entrance were covered with bits of glass and vegetation, straggly trees and bushes, had grown right up to the concrete base of the building. Gradually their roots would crack the foundations.

The elevator was not working, so he had to walk up to the ninth floor. The staircase was cold and dirty and badly lit. Some of the doors stood wide open, revealing rooms just as they had been left, dirty and drafty, with long

cracks in the ceilings and walls. That some of the apartments were still occupied was evident from the smell of
frying and the loud sounds from the morning television
programs. The walls and floors seemed to be completely
without insulation.

Jensen began to breathe more heavily after the fifth
floor and when he reached the ninth, his chest ached and
he had a pain in his right side. After a moment or two, his
breathing grew more even and, taking out his police
badge, he knocked on the door.

The man opened the door at once. He said:

"The police? I am sober and have been so for years."

"Jensen, Chief Inspector from the Sixteenth Division.
I'm carrying out an investigation which concerns your
former post and place of employment."

"Yes?"

"A few questions."

The man shrugged. He was pleasantly dressed and had
a thin face, on which the expression was one of resignation.

"Come in," he said.

The apartment was a standard one, the furniture too.
There was a shelf with a dozen or so books on it, and on
the table stood a cup of coffee, bread, butter, cheese and a
newspaper.

"Please take a seat."

Jensen looked around. The apartment reminded him of
his own. He sat down and took out his pen and notebook.

"When did you terminate your employment?"

"In December last year, just before Christmas."

"You handed in your resignation?"

"Yes."

"You had worked there for a long time?"

"Yes."

"Why did you leave?"

The man took a gulp of coffee. Then he looked at the ceiling. "It's a long story. I don't think it'd interest you much."

"Why did you leave?"

"O.K. I've got nothing to hide, but it's a little difficult to explain what happened."

"Try."

"First of all, the statement that I handed in my resignation is a modification of the truth."

"Explain."

"It would take two days to do so and you still perhaps wouldn't understand. I can only give you a superficial account of the events themselves."

He paused.

"But first I should like to know why. Am I suspected of anything?"

"Yes."

"You won't say what, I suppose?"

"No."

The man rose and went over to the window.

"I came here when this was all newly built," he said. "It wasn't all that long ago. Shortly afterward I was appointed to a job in the concern, almost by accident.

"Before that I worked for another paper, which presumably you don't remember. It was published by the Socialist Party and the Trade Union movement and was the last of the bigger weeklies in the country which was quite independent of the concern. It had certain ambitions, not least cultural ones, though the climate on that particular front was already worsening, even then."

"Cultural ambitions?"

"Yes, it stood for good art and poetry, and it printed literary stories and so on. I'm no expert on those matters. I was a reporter and was occupied with political and social questions."

"Were you a socialist?"

"I was a radical. In fact I was on the extreme left wing of the Socialist Party, though I didn't realize it myself."

"And?"

"The paper was not a very brilliant affair. It didn't make much profit and neither did it run at a loss. A relatively large number of people read it and were dependent on it. It constituted the only opposition to the concern's papers and it fought and criticized the concern and the company, partly actively and partly by its very existence."

"How?"

"Through polemics, editorials, open criticism. By dealing honestly with diverse matters. The company hated it, of course, and hit back in their own way."

"How?"

"By publishing more and more indifferent comic and story magazines, by exploiting people's natural tendencies."

"What tendencies?"

"To prefer looking at pictures to reading and—if they ever read anything—to prefer completely meaningless drivel to something which forces them to think or make an effort or to take a stand. Unfortunately, it was like that even then."

He remained standing by the window with his back to his visitor.

"The phenomenon is called intellectual idleness and is

one of the transient diseases of the television age," said the man.

A jet plane roared over the building in the direction of the airport many miles farther south. From there, every day, huge numbers of people were transported on their annual holiday abroad to some suitably provisioned and chosen place. This activity was organized up to the hilt. Jensen had once gone on one of these trips and he had no intention of doing so again.

"That was at the time when many people still thought that the increase in impotence and frigidity was due to radioactive fallout. Do you remember?"

"Yes."

"Well, the concern couldn't touch our readers. They weren't all that many, but they were united and were people who needed the paper. For them, it was the last straw to clutch. That was probably why the company always loathed us. But they couldn't break us, we thought."

He turned and looked at Jensen.

"This must be all very compromising. I told you it couldn't be explained at the drop of a hat."

"Go on. What happened?"

The man smiled bleakly and went back and sat down on the sofa.

"What happened? The most disconcerting thing you could imagine. Quite simply, they bought us. Neatly and tidily with staff and ideology—the lot. For money. Or if you look at it the other way around, the Party and the Trade Union movement sold us to the opposition."

"Why?"

"That's not easy to explain either. Social equality was

beginning to take shape. It's a long time ago now. Do you know what I think?"

"No."

"At that particular time, socialism in other countries had survived the long crisis and had succeeded in uniting people, as people I mean, making them more free, more secure, activating their personalities, inspiring them to take responsibility . . . We, on our part, were still materially very advanced compared with other countries and the moment to exchange experiences in practice ought therefore to have come. But something quite different occurred. Things developed in another way. Do you find it difficult to follow me?"

"Not at all."

"Here, we were so dazzled by our own excellence, so filled with confidence with the results of so-called practical politics—in broad terms, it was thought that Marxism had been successfully reconciled, almost fused with plutocracy—that socialism became in itself superfluous, something which reactionary theorists had in fact predicted years before. That was also just when the party program began to change. Sections which were considered a threat to social equality were quite simply eliminated. Step by step, practically all the vital principles were yielded. And simultaneously, in the wake of the general grumbling, the moral reactionaries appeared. You see what I'm getting at?"

"Not yet."

"Everywhere, points of view were being pulled nearer and nearer toward each other. Perhaps it was not a bad idea, but the methods used were almost entirely based on keeping quiet about setbacks and difficulties. The problems were lied away. They were smothered by the constantly rising material standard of living, or clouded by meaningless talk which was pumped out via the radio and television. The cover word for this was, then as now, 'harmless entertainment.' The idea was, of course, that the sealed-in infections would meanwhile heal themselves. But that didn't happen. The individual felt himself cared for physically, but spiritually he felt incapacitated, politics and society became something diffuse and incomprehensible, everything was acceptable but uninteresting. Reaction in the individual was first confusion and then gradually indifference. At the root of all this lay this indefinite fear.

"Fear," said the man. "Of what, I don't know. Do you?"

Jensen looked at him expressionlessly.

"Perhaps simply just of living, as always. The absurd thing was that from a superficial point of view, everything was always getting better. There were only three flies in the ointment: alcoholism, the suicides and the birth rate. It was not the thing to mention then, and neither is it now."

He fell silent. Jensen said nothing.

"One of the main principles of social equality, even if it was never clearly formulated or discussed, was that everything must pay for itself. And the terrible thing was that this very doctrine was the fundamental reason for the Trade Union movement and the Party selling us to what we at the time understood to be the arch-enemy. So the motive was quite simply money, not that they wanted to be rid of our freedom of speech and radicalism. They didn't discover the advantages of that until later on."

"And this has embittered you?"

The man did not seem to hear the question.

"But that wasn't the worst humiliation. The worst thing of all was that it was settled without our knowledge, on a level far above us. We had imagined that we mattered, that what we said and what we represented—and the group we represented—meant something, at least sufficient that we would be considered worthy of being told what they were thinking of doing with us. But that wasn't so. The matter was settled between the head of the concern and the leader of the Trade Union movement, by two businessmen around a conference table. Then the Prime Minister and the Party, who arranged some of the practical details, were informed. Those of us who were known and had senior posts were tucked away into sinecures in the management, and others went too. The most unimportant were naturally given the sack. I was one of the middle category. That's what happened, then. It might have been the Middle Ages. For that's what has happened all through the ages. And it showed those of us who had worked there that we had meant nothing whatsoever and were incapable of accomplishing anything. That was the worst of all. It was murder. Murder of an idea."

"And this embittered you?"

"I'm resigned really."

"But your attitude to work became one of hatred? To the concern and its leaders?"

"No, not at all. If you believe that, then you've misunderstood me. They had only behaved quite logically from their point of view. Why should they refuse such an easily bought triumph? Imagine General Hiaja calling

Franco during the battle of Madrid and saying: 'Would you like to buy my planes? They're using too much gas.' Does the comparison tell you anything?"

"No."

"Anyhow, it was an inadequate one. Well, I can give you a simple answer to your question. No, my attitude to the company was not one of hatred, not then, and nor was it so later. I was treated well there."

"But they sacked you?"

"Very humanely, please note. In addition, I myself provoked it."

"How?"

"I deliberately abused their trust, as it's called."

"In what way?"

"I was sent abroad last autumn to collect material for a series of articles. They were to describe a person's life, a man's road to success and wealth. It was about an internationally famous television star, one of those who are constantly forcibly fed to people. That's the kind of thing I've been doing all these years, writing lovely doctored biographies of famous people. But this was the first time I'd been allowed to go to another country to do it."

He smiled his bleak smile again and drummed his fingers on the edge of the table.

"This man, this celebrity, happened to have been born in a socialist country, one of the most carefully ignored ones. I don't think our government had even admitted its existence."

He looked at Jensen with searching and melancholy eyes.

"Do you know what I did? I used the series of articles to make a detailed and thoroughly positive analysis of that country's political and cultural standards, compared with the circumstances here. The articles were naturally not published. I had hardly expected them to be."

He paused briefly and frowned. Then he said:

"The funny thing is I still don't know why I did it."

"Defiance?"

"Possibly. But then, I've not talked to anyone about these things for years. I don't even know why I'm doing so now. I lost the urge after about two weeks in the company, and then I just sat there writing what they wanted, page after page. At first they obviously thought more of me than was justified. They realized I was harmless and might be a useful little cog in the great machine. But then, for the first time, they talked of transferring me to the Special Department. Perhaps you don't know about that?"

"I've heard it mentioned."

"It's called Department Thirty-one. It's considered the most important of all. Why, I can't imagine. One seldom hears it mentioned and the work done there is shrouded in secrecy. It deals with some sort of project, a dummy-group as it's called in the trade. A transfer there was talked about once upon a time, but then they must have realized that the only thing I was any good at was writing nice kindly lives of famous people. They were, in fact, absolutely right."

He absently fingered his coffee-cup.

"And then I suddenly went and did that. God in heaven, were they surprised!"

Jensen nodded.

"You see, I thought I'd never write again and I suddenly couldn't bear the thought of the last thing I wrote being a lying rose-colored sob-story of some bumpkin, a pretty portrait of some moron who earned millions by looking revolting and not being able to sing and who went around the world causing scandals in male brothels."

"The last thing you wrote?"

"Yes, I've given up. I knew long ago that I was written out, that I'd never be able to write again. It came over me all at once. I'll get some quite different work some time, anything. It'll perhaps be a bit difficult, for we journalists can't really do anything. But it'll be all right. Nowadays no one has to be able to do anything, anyhow."

"What do you live on?"

"The company treated me very handsomely. They said they knew I was finished, gave me four months' salary and let me leave at once."

"And you received a diploma?"

The man looked at Jensen in astonishment.

"Yes, I did. Silly, wasn't it? How did you know that?"

"Where is it now?"

"It isn't. I'd like to be able to tell you I tore it up into shreds and flung it out of the thirtieth floor window—but in fact I chucked it away quite prosaically before I left."

"Crumpled up?"

"Otherwise it wouldn't have gone in the waste-paper basket. It was quite large, I remember. Why do you ask?"

Commissioner Jensen asked four more questions.

"Is this your permanent address?"

"As I told you, I've lived here since the building was put up and I'm going to stay as long as the electricity and water remain turned on. In some ways it's better than it used to be. One has no neighbors and so one doesn't notice the lack of insulation."

"Why is the department called the thirty-first?"

"The offices are on the thirty-first floor."

"Is there one?"

"Yes, in the attic, between the comic-strip editorial offices and the roof terrace. The elevators don't go up there."

"Have you ever been there?"

"No, never. Most people in the place don't even know it exists."

Before they parted, the man said:

"I'm sorry I talked so unintelligibly. It must have sounded naïve and confused, as simplified and compressed as that. But you insisted . . ."

And finally:

"By the way, am I still suspected of anything?"

Jensen was already on the stairs and made no reply.

The man stayed standing at the door. He did not look worried, only indifferent and rather tired.

19

He sat for a few moments in the car and looked through his notes. Then he turned the page and wrote: Number 3, ex-editor, 48 years old, unmarried, relieved of post at own request and on full pension.

Number 3 was a woman.

The sun was out, shining brightly and mercilessly. It was Saturday and one minute to twelve. He had exactly thirty-six hours to go. Jensen switched on the starter and drove away.

He had turned off the short-wave set and although he had to drive through the center of the city he did not bother to call in at the Sixteenth Division station.

But he stopped at a cafeteria counter and meditated for a long time on the day's three standard items on the menu. The food was selected by a special department of the Ministry of Health. It was cooked centrally by a large food syndicate and the same dishes were served at all eating places. He stood for so long in front of the electric menu that the line behind him began to get restless.

Then he pressed one of the buttons, took his loaded tray and squeezed in at an empty place at one of the tables.

He sat still and looked at his lunch; milk, carrot juice,

meat loaf, a few strips of white cabbage and two watery potatoes.

He was very hungry but dared not trust his bodily functions. After a moment he took a little bit of the meat, chewed it for a long time, drank the carrot juice, rose and left.

The street he was heading for lay to the east, quite near the center of the city and in a district which had always been inhabited by the temporarily extant upper classes. The building was new and not standard. It belonged to the concern, and except for apartments for visitors and conference halls, it contained a large studio apartment with a terrace and windows in the roof.

The woman who came to the door was small and plump. Her blonde hair was rigidly set and the coating on her face was as smooth and rosy as a colored picture. She was dressed in a partly pink, partly light blue housecoat of some thin light material. On her feet she was wearing red slippers with high heels, gold stitching and strange multicolor pom-poms on the toes.

Jensen seemed to remember an exact replica of this outfit in a pull-out color picture in one of the hundred forty-four magazines.

"Oh, a man!" tittered the woman.

"Jensen, Chief Inspector from the Sixteenth Division. I'm carrying out an investigation which concerns your former post and place of employment," he said in a monotone, holding out his badge.

Meanwhile he was looking past the woman into her apartment.

The room was large and airy and the contents looked expensive. Low furniture made of light-colored woods was arranged against a background of trellis plants and pastel textiles. The whole apartment reminded him of an exaggerated room for the daughter of an American millionaire, transferred lock, stock, and barrel from a store.

Another woman was sitting on the sofa, dark and appreciably younger. On one of the tables was a bottle of sherry, a glass and some kind of cat of exotic origin.

The woman in the housecoat swayed into the room.

"Goodness, how exciting," she said. "A detective."

Jensen followed her in.

"Yes, my dear, a real detective, from some special office or division or whatever it's called. Just like in our magazines."

She turned around and chirped:

"Do sit down, dear man. Please make yourself as comfortable as you can in my little den. Perhaps you'd like a glass of sherry?"

Jensen shook his head and sat down.

"Goodness, I forgot, we're not alone, are we? This is one of my dear colleagues, one of the ones who took over the ship when I went ashore."

The dark woman glanced at Jensen, briefly and without interest. Then she smiled politely and submissively at the woman in the housecoat, who sank down on the sofa, put her head on one side and said in a girlish voice:

"And what can I help you with?"

Jensen took out his notebook and pen.

"When did you give up your job?"

"At the new year. And please, dear man, don't call it a job. To work on a magazine is a vocation, like being a doctor or a priest. One mustn't forget for a moment that one's readers are one's fellow human beings, almost one's spiritual patients. One lives so intensively in the rhythm of the magazine, entirely for the readers, that one has to give oneself to it completely."

The younger woman stared at her shoes and bit her lower lip. The corners of her mouth twitched as if she were trying to suppress a cry or a smile.

"Why did you leave?"

"I left the company because I thought my career had been fulfilled. I had reached my goal. For twenty years I had led the magazine from victory to victory. Yes, I'm not exaggerating when I say I created it with my very own hands. When I took it over it was nothing, absolutely nothing. In a very short time I had made it into the biggest woman's magazine the country."

She looked at the dark woman and said venomously:

"And how did I do it? By working, by sacrificing myself completely. One must live wholly for the task, think in pictures and headlines, with all one's senses open to the demands of the reader, to . . ."

She thought for a moment.

"To satisfy their legitimate needs, to gild their ordinary lives with wonderful dreams, ideals and verses."

She sipped at her sherry and said icily:

"To achieve this, one must have what we call feeling. One must also give one's colleagues feeling. There are not many people who have this natural gift. Sometimes one has to be inwardly very hard to be able to give everything outwardly."

She closed her eyes. Her voice softened.

"All this, one does but with one aim in mind. The magazine and the readers."

"Two," said Inspector Jensen.

The dark woman gave him a swift frightened look. The woman in the housecoat did not react.

"You probably know how I became editor."

"No."

She changed her tone of voice again and said dreamily:

"It's almost like a fairy tale. I see it as a real-life picture story. This is what happened . . ."

Again her voice and expression changed.

"I am of humble origins and am not ashamed to say so," she said aggressively, her nose in the air and the corners of her mouth pulled down.

"Oh yes."

After a swift appraising glance at her visitor, she said positively:

"The Chief of the concern is a genius. Nothing less than a genius. A great man. Greater than Democratus."

"Democratus?"

She tittered and waggled her head.

"Oh, me and names. Naturally I meant someone else. It's not all that easy to keep everything in up there."

Jensen nodded.

"The Chief took me directly from a very humble position and allowed me to take over the magazine. It was an absolutely crazy stroke of daring. Think of me, just a young girl, as head of a large editorial office. But I was the new blood the magazine needed. In three months the place was transformed, I'd cleared out the dead wood and in six months I had made the magazine into the most beloved reading of all women. It's been that ever since."

She changed voice and said, addressing the dark woman:

"Never forget that both the eight-page horoscope and

the cinemascope picture stories and real-life serials on great men's mothers were my ideas. It is still picture-serials that do the trick. And the pet's supplement in four colors."

She made a swift dismissive gesture with her glittering beringed fingers and said placidly:

"But I'm not telling you all this to win praise and flattery. I've already received my reward in the form of hundreds of thousands of heart-warming letters from grateful readers."

The woman sat in silence for a moment, with her hand still raised and her head to one side, as if she had fixed her eyes on to the distant horizon.

"Don't ask me how one brings such things about," she said modestly. "One just simply feels; one feels it just as certainly as one knows that every woman at least once in her life wants to experience a warm, intense look, full of desire . . ."

The dark-haired woman let out a muffled gurgling sound.

The woman in the housecoat started and stared at her with undisguised loathing.

"That was, of course, in our day," she said patronizingly, "when we women still had a little fire in our pants."

Her face had fallen and a network of lines had appeared around her eyes and mouth. She bit irritably at her left thumbnail, which was long, pointed, and silvered.

"You received a diploma when you left?"

"Oh yes," she said. "Oh, it was terribly nice."

The teenage smile came back and her eyes began to sparkle.

"Would you like to see it?"

"Yes."

She rose gracefully and floated away. The dark woman threw a panic-stricken look at Jensen.

The woman came back with the document pressed to her bosom.

"And just fancy, every single person of importance has signed it, even a royal princess."

She opened the folder. The blank left page was covered with signatures.

"I think this was the loveliest thing of all, out of all the hundreds of presents I had. From all over the place. Wouldn't you like to see them?"

"It won't be necessary," said Jensen.

The woman smiled, shy and bewildered.

"But why have you come, a Chief Inspector of the Police, asking me questions about all this?"

"I am not in a position to discuss the matter," said Jensen.

Her face went through a series of swiftly changing expressions. Then she spread out her hands, helpless and feminine, and said submissively:

"Yes, well then, I'll have to submit myself . . ."

The dark woman accompanied him down. The elevator had hardly started when the girl sniffed and said:

"Don't believe a word she says. She's terrible, frightful, a monster. There are the most awful stories about her."

"Oh yes."

"She's a masterpiece of malice and prying. She still holds all the strings, although they managed to get her out of the building. Now she's forcing me to spy for her. Every Wednesday and Saturday, I have to come here and give a complete report. She wants to know absolutely everything."

"Why do you do it?"

"Oh, my God, why? She could crush me in about ten minutes, just as you squash a louse. She wouldn't hesitate for a moment. And she insults me all the time. Oh, my God."

Jensen said nothing. When they reached the ground floor, he raised his hat and opened the doors. The young woman gave him a timid look and half ran out to the street.

The traffic had thinned out noticeably. It was Saturday and five to four. He had a pain in the right side of his diaphragm.

20

Jensen had switched off the ignition but was still sitting with his notebook open on the steering-wheel. He had just written: Number 4, art editor, unmarried, 20 years old, left at own request.

Number 4 was also a woman.

The building was on the other side of the street. It was not absolutely new but was well maintained. He found the right door on the ground floor and pressed the bell. No one came. He rang again several times and then knocked loudly. In the end he tried the door-handle. The door was locked. There was not a sound from inside. He remained standing outside the door for a few minutes. Meanwhile the telephone began ringing in the apartment. He went back to the car, turned over five pages of the notebook and wrote: Number 5, 52 years old, journalist, unmarried, period of employment terminated according to contract. This time he was in luck. The street was in the same district and he only had to drive five blocks farther on.

The building was similar to the one he had visited ten minutes before, a long yellow five-story building, placed at an angle to the street. The whole of this part of the city contained similar blocks.

The label on the door consisted of letters cut out of a newspaper and taped on to the glass window. Some of them had become torn and some had fallen away, making the name illegible. The bell worked but although he could hear someone moving about in the apartment, a few minutes elapsed before anyone came to the door.

The man was older than he had expected. And he was remarkably unkempt, with long rumpled hair and a wild gray beard. He was wearing a soiled yellow-white shirt, baggy trousers and down-at-the-heel black shoes. Jensen frowned. Badly dressed people were very rare nowadays.

"Jensen, Chief Inspector from the Sixteenth Division. I'm carrying out an investigation which concerns your former post and place of employment."

"Can you identify yourself?" the man said immediately.

Jensen showed him the enamel badge.

"Come in," said the man.

His manner was self-confident, bordering on arrogance.

The disorder in the apartment was remarkable. The floor was covered with newspapers, magazines, books, old oranges, pieces of paper, refuse bags stuffed full, dirty clothes, and unwashed crocks. The furniture consisted of a few wooden chairs, two tattered armchairs, a rickety table and an unmade sofa bed. One half of the table had been cleared to accommodate a typewriter and a heap of completed manuscript. Over everything lay a thick layer of gray dust. The atmosphere was musty. And there was a smell of drink. The man swept the other half of the table clear with a folded newspaper. The indefinite heap of paper, household articles and rubbish crashed to the floor.

"Sit here," he said, pushing up a chair.

"You're drunk," said Jensen.

"Not drunk. Under the influence. I'm never drunk but mostly under the influence. The difference is considerable."

Jensen sat down. The bearded man stood slightly behind him.

"You're observant," he said, "otherwise you would never have noticed. Hardly anyone ever notices."

"When did you leave your job?"

"Two months ago. Why do you ask?"

Jensen put his spiral notebook down on the table and leafed through it. When page number 3 came up, the man behind him said:

"I'm in very good company."

Jensen went on turning the pages.

"I'm surprised you got away from that ghastly bitch with your reason intact," said the man, walking around the table. "Did you go to her place? I'd never dare do that."

"You know her?"

"Do I know her! I was working on the magazine when she arrived. When she became editor. And I survived almost a whole year."

"Survived?"

"I was, of course, much younger and stronger then."

He sat down on the bed, thrust his right hand into the heap of dirty bedclothes and pulled out a bottle.

"As you noticed anyhow, it doesn't matter, does it?" he said. "And I don't get drunk. Only more incisive."

Jensen looked steadily at him.

The man took a couple of gulps out of the bottle, put it down and said:

"What are you after?"

"Certain information."

"Concerning what?"

Jensen did not reply.

"If you want to know something about that damn bitch, you've come to the right place. Very few people know her as well as I do. I could write her biography."

The man fell silent but did not seem to be expecting an answer. He looked at his visitor with his eyes half closed, then at the window, almost opaque with dirt. In spite of the drink, his eyes were watchful and observant.

"Do you know how she became the editor of the biggest magazine in the country?"

Jensen said nothing.

"Pity," said the man thoughtfully. "Far too few people know about it. And yet it was one of the greatest turning points in the history of the Press."

Silence fell in the room. Jensen looked indifferently at the man and rolled his plastic pen between his fingers.

"Do you know what her occupation was before she became editor?"

He laughed nastily.

"Cleaner. And do you know where she did her cleaning?"

Jensen drew a very small five-pointed star on the empty page of his notebook.

"In the holy of holies. On the directors' floor. How she succeeded in getting just there, I don't know, but you can be quite certain it was not a matter of chance."

He bent down and picked up the bottle.

"She could fix anything. You see, she was nice-looking, hellishly nice—one thought until one had known her for five minutes."

He drank.

"At that time the cleaning began after office hours. At

six o'clock, the cleaners arrived. All of them, except her.
She was there an hour earlier and then the Chief was
usually in his room. He used to send the secretarial staff
away on the dot of five and then sit messing about with
something he didn't want anyone else to see. What, I don't
know.

"But I can imagine," he said, looking toward the
window.

The room had grown dark. Jensen looked at his watch.
It was a quarter past six.

"At exactly quarter past five she would open the door
to his room and look in, say sorry and shut it again. When
he was about to leave or go to the cloakroom or somewhere
else, he always saw her disappearing around a corner of the
corridor."

Jensen opened his mouth to say something but at once
changed his mind.

"She was especially nice-looking from behind, you see.
I remember what she looked like very well. She wore a
light blue overall and white wooden-soled slippers and a
white kerchief around her head, and she was always bare-
legged. Presumably she'd heard some talk—I remember
it was said that the Chief could not resist the backs of
knees."

The man rose, took a few shuffling steps and switched on
the light.

"This hadn't gone on for long before the Chief began
to bump into her. He was known to be hot on this point.
It's said that he always begins by introducing himself, oddly
enough. But do you know what happened?"

The bulb in the ceiling had been covered with a greasy
cloth and gave out a weak uncertain light.

"She did not answer at first, just timidly mumbled something incomprehensible and stared at him with doe-like eyes. All the time, she carried on as before."

Jensen drew another star. Six-pointed.

"She became an obsession with him. He did everything possible. Tried to get hold of her home address. No good. God knows where she had tucked herself away. They say he had people tail her, but she outwitted them. Then she began coming a quarter of an hour later. He was still there. She came even later and he was usually sitting in his room, pretending to be busy with something. And then in the end . . ."

He fell silent. Jensen waited for thirty seconds. Then he raised his eyes and looked blankly at the man on the bed.

"He went completely off his rocker, you see. One evening, she didn't come until half-past eight, when all the other cleaners had finished and gone home. The lights were out in his room but she knew he was there because she had seen his hat and coat. So she walked up and down the corridor once or twice, banging with her wooden shoes and then took her damn bucket and went in and shut the door behind her."

He chuckled to himself quietly.

"It was wonderful," he said. "The Chief was standing behind the door, wearing nothing but an undershirt, and he jumped on her with a yell and tore her clothes off, upsetting the bucket, throwing her to the floor and sitting on her. She fought back squealing and . . ."

The man stopped and looked triumphantly at his visitor.

"And what do you think happened?"

Jensen was looking at something on the floor. It was impossible to tell whether he were listening.

"Well, just at that very moment, a uniformed nightwatchman came in with his bunch of keys and shone his flashlight straight on them. When he saw who it was, he was simply petrified and slammed the door and ran away, with the Chief running after him. The night-watchman rushed into an elevator and the Chief just got in after him before the doors closed. He thought the night-watchman was going to sound the alarm—but the poor devil was only absolutely scared stiff he'd lose his job. She of course had calculated the whole thing and knew to the second when he usually went on his rounds to clock the time on the control clocks."

The man gurgled with suppressed laughter and wriggled delightedly in the tangle of bedclothes.

"Just think, the Chief was in the elevator with nothing on but his undershirt, together with a paralyzed nightwatchman in full uniform and peaked cap and with flashlight and truncheon and huge bunch of keys and the lot. They rode all the way down to the storeroom before one of them could bring himself to press the stop button and reverse the elevator and then they rode all the way back up again. And when they got there, the nightwatchman wasn't a night-watchman any longer, but an inspector of the entire building, and he had become so in spite of not daring to say a single word the whole time."

The man fell silent. The glow in his eyes seemed to die. He said resignedly:

"The old inspector got the sack for appointing such poor staff."

"Yes, well, then the day of reckoning came and she must

have called the tune, because a week later an inter-office message arrived to say that our editor had been dismissed and a quarter of an hour later, she swept into the office and all hell let loose."

The man seemed suddenly to remember the bottle and took a careful little sip.

"You see, the magazine was quite good, but it wasn't selling well. Although it only dealt with princesses and how to make gingersnaps, it was above the readers' heads, or so it was said, and there'd been talk of closing it down. But . . ."

He looked penetratingly at his visitor, as if trying to make contact, but Jensen did not meet his eyes.

"She set about it like a night of the long knives. Practically all the staff were cleared out and replaced by the most fantastic morons. We had an editorial secretary who was really a hairdresser and had never seen a semicolon in her life. When she happened to see one on her typewriter, she came and asked me what it was—and I was so frightened of getting the sack that I didn't dare tell her. I remember saying that it was probably some intellectual horror of some sort."

He munched for a moment with his toothless jaws.

"That damn bitch hated everything that was intellectual, you see, and when she was allowed to say it herself, practically everything was intellectual, especially being able to write coherent sentences on a piece of paper. Another reason for my survival was that 'I didn't seem to be like the others.' And that I watched every word I ever said. I remember a newly appointed reporter was stupid enough to tell a story about one of the other editors, to curry favor. It was in fact an authentic episode and also damn funny.

Apparently a man from the ideas department went up to the cultural editor of one of the larger magazines and said that August Strindberg was a hell of a good author and that his film "Miss Julie" would make a hit as a comic strip, if it was rewritten a bit and class differences and that sort of nonsense taken out. The cultural editor thought and then said: 'What did you say the man's name was?' And the ideas fellow said: 'August Strindberg, you know.' And then the cultural editor said: 'Hell, yes, of course. Well, tell him to come to the Grand tomorrow at twelve and we'll have lunch and discuss fees.' This reporter then, told this story and she just looked icily at him and said: 'What's so funny about that?' And two hours later, he had to take his money and go."

The man began to chuckle again. Jensen raised his eyes and looked at him blankly.

"But now this is really it. By her quite outstanding stupidity, she succeeded in doubling the circulation in six months. The magazine was filled with pictures of dogs and children and cats and potted-plants, and with horoscopes and phrenology and how one tells fortunes in coffee dregs and how one waters geraniums and there wasn't a single comma in the right place, but people bought it. You see, the little bit which might be described as text was so unbelievably simplified and naïve that it was comparable to what is written today. One wasn't allowed to write locomotive without explaining that it was an apparatus on wheels which ran on iron rails and pulled carriages behind it. And for the Chief it was the great determining victory. Everyone said that his daring and foresight had been quite unique and it was a maneuver which revolutionized all journalistic training and altered the very principles of modern publishing."

He took another sip from the bottle.

"It was perfect. The only fly in the ointment was the night-watchman. He was fearfully proud of his new position and couldn't keep quiet about how he got it. But he wasn't allowed to talk for long. Six months later he was crushed to death in the service elevator. It stopped between two floors and he got out to get it going again. He was practically chopped in half. He was so stupid that one can say with some justification that it was his own fault."

The man put his hand to his mouth and coughed raucously for some time. When the attack had passed, he said:

"And then she just went on, year after year. She got more and more refined. God help us, more and more pretentious and the paper got more and more spattered with pictures of unwearable clothes. They said the manufacturers bribed her. In the end they managed to get rid of her after all, but it wasn't cheap. The Chief is said to have had to put down fifty thousand in cash to get her to retire on full salary."

"Why did you leave?" said Jensen.

"What does that matter?"

"Why did you leave?"

The bottle was empty. The man shook himself and said roughly: "I was chucked out. Just like that. Without a penny's compensation, after all those years."

"For what reason?"

"They wanted to get rid of me. I didn't look nice enough, I suppose. I was not a worthy ambassador of the company.

And I've written myself out. Can't write a word any more, not even tripe. It happens to everyone."

"Was this the actual reason?"

"No."

"What was the actual reason for your dismissal?"

"I was caught drinking in my room."

"And you had to leave at once?"

"Yes. Officially, of course, I wasn't dismissed. My contract was so written that it gave them the right to chuck me out when they liked."

"And you didn't protest?"

"No."

"Why not?"

"It would have been pointless. They had succeeded in appointing a personnel manager who had been the leader of the journalists' union before and who still ran it. He knows every corner and no ordinary mortal stands a chance. If one appeals, one has to do it to him indirectly and then he makes the decision. It's clever, but it's the same in everything. Their tax lawyers are employed at the Ministry of Finance at the same time. Any criticism directed toward the weeklies, once in five years, they write themselves in their own dailies. But it's like that with everything."

"Did this embitter you?"

"I don't think so. I'm past that now. Whoever is embittered nowadays?"

"Did you get a kind of diploma when you left?"

"Possibly. Very nice too. The personnel manager is an expert at that kind of thing. He smiles and offers you a cigar with one hand and strangles you with the other. And he looks like a toad."

The man's concentration seemed to waver.

"You received a diploma, didn't you?"

"What does that matter?"

"You received a diploma, didn't you?"

"I think so."

"Have you still got it?"

"I don't know."

"Show it to me."

"I neither can nor wish to."

"Is it here in the apartment?"

"I don't know. And even if it were, I couldn't find it. Would you be able to find anything here?"

Jensen looked around. Then he closed his notebook and rose.

"Good-bye," he said.

"You still haven't told me why you came here."

Jensen did not reply. He picked up his hat and left the room. The man remained seated among his dirty bedclothes. He looked gray and worn and his eyes were troubled.

Jensen switched on the car radio, called up a police bus and left the address.

"Yes," he said. "Drunkenness in the home. Take him to the main station in the Sixteenth Division. It's urgent."

There was a telephone booth on the other side of the street. He went across and called the head of the Civil Patrol.

"House search. It's urgent. You know what to look for."

"Yes, sir."

"Then go back to the station and wait. Keep him there until you get further orders."

"On what pretext?"

"Any."

"Right."

Jensen went back to his car. After driving fifty yards he met the police bus.

21

Light was trickling through the mail box. Jensen took out his notebook and again read what he had written: Number 4, art editor, 20 years old, unmarried, left at own request. Then he put the notebook back in his pocket, took out his badge and pressed the bell.

"Who is it?"

"Police."

"Nonsense. I've told you, once and for all, it's no good. I don't want to."

"Open up."

"Never. I don't want to."

"Open up."

"Go away. For God's sake leave me alone. Tell him I don't want to."

Jensen banged twice on the door.

"Police. Open up."

The door swung open and she stared suspiciously at him.

"No," she said. "Now this is really going too far, damn it all."

He stepped through the door and showed his badge.

"Jensen," he said. "Chief Inspector from the Sixteenth

Division. I'm carrying out an investigation which concerns your former post and place of employment."

She stared at the enamel badge and retreated backward into the apartment.

The woman was young, with dark hair, deep gray eyes and a firm chin-line. She was dressed in a checked shirt, khaki trousers, and rubber boots. She was long-legged and slim-waisted, but with broad hips. When she moved, he could see she was not wearing anything under her shirt. Her hair was short and untidy and she obviously did not use cosmetics.

In some way she reminded him of women in pictures of the old days.

Her look was difficult to interpret. It seemed to reflect anger, fear, desperation, all in equal parts.

Her trousers were spattered with paint and she was holding a brush in her hand. Several newspapers lay spread out over the floor and in the middle of them stood a rocking chair which she had been painting.

Jensen looked around. The furniture all seemed as if it had been found on a rubbish dump by someone and then painted in bright colors.

"Then you weren't lying," she said. "So he's even gone and put the police on me. This really is the limit. You can't frighten me. Lock me up, by all means, if you can find some pretext. I've got a bottle of wine in the kitchen—perhaps that'll do. It doesn't matter. Anything would be better than things as they are."

Jensen took out his notebook.

"When did you leave your job?"

"Two weeks ago. I just didn't go back. Is that illegal?"

"How long had you been employed by the concern?"

"Two weeks. Have you got any more stupid questions to plague me with? I've told you it's no good."

"Why did you leave?"

"Good God, why do you think? Because I couldn't stand being pestered every moment of my life and being chased every step I took."

"You were the art director?"

"Not on your life. I was an assistant in the lay-out department. Glue-girl, it's usually called. I never even had time to learn anything properly before this crazy situation arose."

"What does being an art editor entail?"

"Heaven only knows. I think one sits and designs lettering and copies pages out of foreign papers."

"Exactly why did you leave your job?"

"Good God in heaven, do they control the police too? Have you no pity for me? Give my regards to your boss and tell him that there are sure to be clinics which would suit him far better than my bed."

"Why did you leave?"

"I left because I couldn't stand it. Can't you try to understand? He spotted me almost at once. A photographer I knew had gotten me to model for a picture for some medical investigation. And he had seen the photograph. I went with him to some peculiar little restaurant, miles away from respectability. Then I let him come here, idiot that I was. The night after, he called up—*he called me,* that is—and asked if I had a bottle of wine at home. I told him to go to hell. And then it went on."

She was standing with her feet apart in the middle of the room, staring at him.

"What in heaven's name do you want to know? That he

sat on the floor over there and babbled away for three hours holding on to my foot? And that he nearly had a stroke when I finally tore myself free and went to bed?"

"You're giving me a great deal of superfluous information."

She flung the brush away and several splashes of red paint fell on the floor.

"Yes, yes," she said nervously. "I'd probably have slept with him if it had been that way. Why not? One has to try to show some interest in something. I was sleepy of course, but how was I to know he'd pass out just because I got undressed? Don't you see what hell it's been these last weeks, day in day out? He must have me. He must have my simple natural instincts. He will send me all over the world. I must help him find something which has been lost. He'll make me head of God knows what. Head—me! No, darling, you don't have to be able to do anything. Not interested? That doesn't matter, darling."

"I repeat, you're giving me a great deal of superfluous information."

She drew in her breath and frowned at him.

"Haven't you come . . . didn't he send you?"

"No. You received some kind of diploma when you left?"

"Yes, but . . ."

"Show it to me."

Her eyes were full of curiosity and nothing more. She went over to a blue desk standing against one wall, opened a drawer and took out the diploma.

"It doesn't look too good," she said uncertainly.

Jensen opened the folder. Someone had added large red exclamation marks to the gold lettering. On the inside of the cover were several obscene sketches, also scribbled in red.

"Of course, one shouldn't do such things, but I was simply furious. It was laughable. I hadn't been there more than two weeks and all I had done was to allow my foot to be held for three hours, and undressed and put on my pajamas."

Jensen put his notebook into his pocket.

"Good-bye," he said.

Just as he was stepping into the hall, the pain in his stomach caught him. It came swiftly and very violently. Everything swam before his eyes and taking an uncertain step forward, he leaned against the doorpost.

She was there at once.

"What's the matter?" she said. "Are you ill? Come and sit down for a moment. I'll help you."

He stayed where he was and he felt her body. She was close to him, supporting him.

"Wait," she said. "I'll get some water."

She ran out into the kitchen and returned at once.

"Look, drink this. Can I do anything? Wouldn't you like to rest a little? I'm sorry I behaved like that. You see, I misunderstood you completely. One of them up there, I won't say which, has been after me all the time."

Jensen straightened up. The pain was still just as severe, but he had already begun to get used to it.

"I'm sorry," she said. "But I didn't realize what you wanted. I still don't know, for that matter. Oh, everything goes wrong. I'm so frightened sometimes, that there's something wrong with me, that I'm different. But I want to take an interest in something and make my own decisions. I was different at school too, and no one understood when I asked about things. I was only interested. I was different, not like other women. I'm always noticing it. It's true. I look different too, and I even smell different. Either I'm mad or the world is, and one's just as bad as the other."

The pain gradually began to give way.

"You should watch your tongue," said Chief Inspector Jensen.

He picked up his hat and went out to the car.

22

As Jensen drove into the city, he contacted the duty-officer at the Sixteenth Division. The men on the search had not yet returned. The Chief of Police had tried to get him several times during the day.

When he reached the center of the city, it was already past eleven o'clock, the traffic had thinned out and there were only a few pedestrians on the sidewalks. The pain in his stomach had slackened and was now only the usual stubborn grinding. His mouth was dry and as always after an attack, he was thirsty. He stopped at one of the few cafeterias still open and ordered a bottle of mineral water. The place glittered with chromium and mirrors. It was empty except for six youngsters in their late teens who were staring apathetically ahead in silence. The waiter was yawning and reading one of the hundred forty-four magazines, a comic strip. Three television sets were showing a harmless program with thunderous synchronized mechanical laughter.

He drank the mineral water slowly, in short sips, and he felt the liquid dissolving the churning bubbling chain reactions in his empty stomach. A moment later he rose and went to the cloakroom. In the urinal, a well-dressed middle-aged man was lying flat on his back with one arm in the drain. He reeked of alcohol and had vomited all over his jacket and shirt. His eyes were open but blank and unseeing.

Jensen went back to the counter.

"There's a drunk in the urinal," he said.

The waiter shrugged his shoulders and went on letting his eyes skim along the rows of colored pictures.

Jensen showed his badge. The man at once put the magazine down and went over to the police-telephone. All restaurants had direct communications with the radio-headquarters of the nearest police station.

The constables who came to get the drunk looked exhausted. As they carried the man out, they struck his head several times against the imitation marble floor. They had come from another division, probably the Eleventh, and did not recognize Jensen.

It was five to twelve when the waiter glanced apologetically at his customer and began to shut down. Jensen went out to the car and called up the duty-officer at the Sixteenth Division station. The search patrol had just returned.

"Yes," said the head of the Civil Patrol. "We found it."

"Intact?"

"Yes, as much of the pages as there were. There was, of course, a flattened sausage between them."

Jensen sat silently for a moment.

"It took a long time," said the head of the Civil Patrol, "but it wasn't all that easy. What a garbage dump. Thousands of bits of paper."

"See to it that the man is released in the usual way early tomorrow morning."

"Right."

"One more thing."

"Yes, sir."

"A few years ago, the building inspector at the company was killed in an elevator."

"Yes."

"Look into the circumstances. Find out what you can about the man, especially his family situation. It's urgent."

"Right. Sir?"

"Yes."

"I understand the Chief of Police has been looking for you."

"Did he leave a message?"

"Not as far as I know."

"Good night."

He hung up. Somewhere in the vicinity a clock struck twelve with harsh penetrating clangs.

The sixth day had gone. Exactly twenty-four hours of his respite remained.

23

Jensen took the drive home quietly. He was physically tired but knew he would find it very hard to get to sleep. And he had not many hours left.

He did not meet a single vehicle in the long tunnel, which was whitewashed and clearly lit, and farther south the great industrial area lay silent and abandoned. The aluminum tanks and plastic roofs of the factories glimmered in the moonlight.

On the bridge he was overtaken by a police bus and a moment later by an ambulance, both driving very fast with their sirens on.

Halfway along the highway he had to stop at a police barrier. The constable with a flashlight recognized him; when Jensen rolled down the car window, the man came to attention and said:

"Road accident. One dead. The wreckage is blocking the road. We'll have it cleared in a few minutes."

Jensen nodded. He sat with the window open and let the raw night air stream into the car. As he waited, he thought about road accidents, the numbers of which were falling year by year, while the number of deaths in traffic was constantly rising. The experts in the Ministry of Communications had long since solved this statistical riddle. The fall in the number of collisions and amount of material damage could to some extent be explained by the better roads and more vigorous traffic control. But the psychological factor was more important; people had become dependent on their cars. They handled them more carefully and reacted more or less subconsciously to the thought of being deprived of them. The rising number of deaths was due to several fatalities which should really be counted as suicides. Here too, the psychological factors played a large part. People lived with and for their cars and also wanted to die in them. This had been shown in an investigation which had been made several years earlier. It had been marked secret, but senior police officers had been given the opportunity to see it.

The road was cleared in eight minutes, so he rolled up the window and drove on. The road surface was covered with a light film of frost, and at the place where the accident had happened, the tire marks were clearly visible. They had not been made by skidding or braking, but led straight toward a concrete post on the side of the road. The insurance claim would probably not be honored. But there was also the possibility that the driver had been tired and had fallen asleep at the wheel.

Jensen felt vaguely dissatisfied, as if something were missing. When he tried to analyze the feeling, he became aware of piercing hunger. He parked the car in front of the seventh block in the third row, went over to an automat and pressed the button for a package of synthetic dietetic gruel.

Up in the apartment, he hung up his coat and his jacket, and switched on the light. Then he drew the blinds, went into the kitchen, measured out half a pint of water into a saucepan and whipped the gruel powder into it. When it was hot, he poured it into a cup and took it back to his room, put the cup on the bedside table, sat down on the bed and undid his shoelaces. It was quarter past two and the building was completely silent. He was still conscious that something was missing.

He got the spiral notebook from his jacket, switched on the lamp by his bed and switched off the overhead light. As he sipped the gruel, he slowly and systematically read through his notes. The gruel was thick and gluey and tasted musty and stale.

When he had finished reading, he raised his eyes and looked at the framed photographs from the police college. He himself featured in one photograph, last but one on the right in the back row. He was standing with his arms folded and a blurred smile on his face. Evidently he had said something to the friend next to him just as the photograph had been taken.

After a moment, he got up and went out into the hall. He opened the cupboard door and took out one of the bottles lying in a row behind his uniform caps on the hat shelf. Then he got a tumbler from the kitchen, filled it and put it down on the bedside table with the gruel cup.

He unfolded the list of nine names and put it down in front of him on the table. He sat absolutely still and looked at it.

The electric wall-clock in the kitchen struck the hour with three short pings.

Jensen turned over a new page in the spiral notebook and wrote: Number 6, 38 years old, divorced, public relations, transferred to other activities.

When he had noted the address, he shook his head almost imperceptibly.

Then he set the alarm clock, put out the light and undressed. He put on his pajamas and sat on the bed with the blankets over his knees. The gruel seemed to be swelling in his stomach, as if something were pressing from below on his heart.

He picked up the tumbler and emptied it in two draughts. The sixty-proof liquor burned his tongue and sank like a column of fire down his throat.

He lay on his back in the dark and waited to relax.

24

Jensen did not sleep. Between three o'clock and twenty past five, he lay in a stupor, incapable of either thinking clearly or switching off his thoughts. When the alarm went off, he was feeling sick and was soaked with sweat. Forty minutes later, he was sitting in the car.

The place he was heading for lay a hundred forty miles to the north and as it was Sunday, he calculated that it would take him three hours to drive there.

The city was silent and deserted, with its empty multistory garages and vacant parking places, but the traffic lights were still functioning as usual, and during the journey through the center of the city he had to stop ten times for the red lights.

The highway was straight and good and the countryside on each side uninteresting. Here and there, he could see suburbs in the distance, silhouetted against the sky. Between the horizon and the highway lay dry and desolate vegetation consisting of deformed trees and low straggly bushes.

At eight o'clock, Jensen pulled in to a gas station to fill up. He also drank a mug of lukewarm tea and made two telephone calls.

The head of the Civil Patrol sounded tired and hoarse, having obviously just woken up.

"It happened nineteen years ago," he said. "The man was caught in an elevator and crushed to death."

"Did you look into the details of the case?"

"There was only a routine investigation in the records. The case was obviously quite straightforward. Pure accident, it was thought, a temporary break in the current which halted the elevator mechanism for a few minutes and then set it going again on its own. And the man was evidently very careless."

"And next-of-kin?"

"He had no family. Lived in a bachelor hotel."

"Did he leave anything?"

"Yes. In fact, under the circumstances, quite a large sum of money."

"Who inherited it?"

"No next-of-kin came forward within the prescribed time. The money finally went to some state fund."

"Anything else?"

"Nothing that seemed important. The man was a lone bird, lived alone, had no friends."

"Good-bye."

The man who was searching in the newspaper records was also at home.

"Jensen here."

"Yes, sir."

"Any results?"

"Haven't you received my report, sir?"

"No."

"I took it in yesterday morning."

"Report verbally."

"Yes, sir," said the man. "One moment while I try to remember."

"Yes."

"The letters used in the anonymous letter came from the same newspaper, but they were not all cut out on the same day. They were taken from two different issues, the Friday edition and the Saturday edition of the previous week. The type is called Bodoni."

Jensen took out his notebook and wrote the information down on the inside of the cover.

"Anything else?"

The man was silent for a moment. Then he said:

"Yes, one other thing. The correct combination of letters to text on the back did not appear in all the editions of the paper. It was only in the so-called A-edition."

"Which means?"

"It means that the letters were only in the newspapers that were printed last. The ones that are sent out to news-agents and subscribers here in the city."

"You're released from the case," said Jensen. "Return to normal duties. Good-bye."

He replaced the receiver, went out to the car and drove on.

At nine o'clock he passed a deserted high-density area consisting of a thousand or so identical blocks of apartments, grouped in a rectangle around a factory. Thick yellowish columns of smoke were rising from the factory chimneys. Two or three hundred feet up, the cloud of gases flattened out and slowly sank back over the town.

A quarter of an hour later he was there.

His estimate had been correct. The stop at the filling station had taken approximately fifteen minutes.

The house was a modern cottage with glass walls and a corrugated plastic roof. It stood on a slope about two miles east of the highway and was surrounded by trees. At the bottom of the slope lay a lake of gray-brown water. The air was polluted with the smell from the factory.

On the concrete square in front of the house stood a plump man in a dressing-gown and slippers. He seemed listless and haggard and looked at his visitor without enthusiasm. Jensen showed his police badge.

"Jensen, Chief Inspector from the Sixteenth Division. I am carrying out an investigation which concerns your former post and place of employment."

"What do you want?"

"A few questions."

"Come in then," he said.

The two rooms contained rugs, ashtrays and tubular furniture which looked as if they had all been taken straight from the company building.

Jensen took out his notebook and pen.

"When did you leave your job?"

The other man yawned deliberately and looked around as if he wished to evade something.

"Three months ago," he said finally.

"Why did you leave?"

The man looked at Jensen. There was a thoughtful glint in his deep gray eyes. He seemed to be considering whether to answer or not. Eventually he made a vague gesture and said:

"If it's the diploma you want to see, I haven't got it here."

Jensen said nothing.

"It's still at my . . . at my wife's apartment in town."

"Why did you leave?"

The man frowned, as if trying to concentrate. After a while, he said:

"Look, whatever you've heard and whatever you think, then you're wrong. I can't help you with anything."

"Why did you leave your job?"

There was silence for a few seconds. The man rubbed the end of his nose unhappily.

"I haven't really left. My contract with the company did run out, but I'm still connected with the concern."

"What is your work now?"

Jensen looked around the bare room. The other man followed his gaze. After a renewed silence, longer than the one before, the man said:

"Look, what's the good of this? I know absolutely nothing that would be of any use to you. I swear that that diploma is still at the apartment in town."

"Why should I want to see your diploma?"

"I don't know. It seems odd you've driven a hundred and forty miles for a thing like that."

The man shook his head.

"How long did it take you by the way?"

He said this with a slight show of interest, but Jensen did not reply and the man returned to his earlier tone of voice.

"My best time was an hour and fifty-eight minutes," he said gloomily.

"Do you have a telephone here?"

"No, there isn't one."

"Do you own this house?"

"No."

"Who owns it?"

"The concern. It's been lent to me. I'm having a rest before taking up a new job."

"What job?"

The replies were becoming more and more hesitant. Now they seemed to cease altogether.

"Do you like it here?"

The man looked appealingly at Jensen.

"Look, I keep telling you, you've got it all wrong. I've nothing to say that could be the slightest use to you. All those stories are quite irrelevant, believe you me."

"What stories?"

"Well, whatever it is you've heard."

Jensen looked steadily at him. There was complete silence. The smell from the factory was just as strong in the house as it had been outside.

"What position did you hold in the concern?"

"Oh, all sorts. Sportswriter, primarily. Then I was editor of a couple of magazines. Then I went in to the ad department. Traveled a lot, mostly reporting sporting events all over the world. Then I was in the overseas office and then . . . well, I traveled around studying."

"What did you study?"

"All kinds of things. Public relations and things like that."

"What does public relations involve?"

"That's not easy to explain."

"So you're widely traveled?"

"I've been almost everywhere."

"Are you good at languages?"

"We-ell, I don't find languages exactly easy."

Jensen sat in silence for a while. He did not take his eyes off the man in the dressing-gown. Finally he said:

"Do the newspapers often publish sports stories?"

"No."

The man looked unhappier than ever.

"No one is interested in sports nowadays, except on television."

"And yet you went around the world reporting on sports events?"

"I've never been able to write about anything else. I tried, but it didn't work."

"Why did you leave?"

"I was too expensive, I think."

The man thought for a few seconds.

"In spite of everything, they are pretty mean," he said, looking solemnly at the tubular furniture.

"What postal district are we in?"

The man looked irresolutely at Jensen. Then he made a gesture toward the window. Above the woods on the other side of the lake lay a cloud of yellow smoke from the factory.

"Same as that . . . the mailman comes from there, anyhow."

"Do you get mail here every day?"

"Not on Sundays."

There was not a sound except that of the man's breathing and the distant roar of traffic on the highway.

"Must you go on plaguing me like this? It's serving no useful purpose."

"Do you know why I've come here?"

"No idea."

The man in the dressing-gown fidgeted uneasily. The silence seemed to trouble him.

"I'm just an ordinary fellow who has had a bit of bad luck, that's all," he said.

"Bad luck?"

"Yes. Bad luck. Everyone says it's exactly the opposite. But you can see for yourself. Here I am, moldering away, lonely. What's lucky about that?"

"What do you want to do?"

"Nothing. I don't want to be any trouble to anyone."

The silence became drawn out and oppressive. Twice the man in the dressing-gown looked appealingly at Jensen but both times immediately turned his eyes away again.

"Please go away now," he said in muffled tones. "I swear that the diploma is in town. In my wife's apartment."

"You don't seem to like it here."

"I didn't say so."

"Didn't you like your job?"

"Of course I did. Why shouldn't I? They gave me everything I wanted there."

He seemed to sink into futile brooding. Finally he said:

"You've misunderstood everything. You've heard those stories and now you think something, but I don't know what. And anyhow, it's not as people say. It quite simply is not true. Not all of it, anyhow."

"So what is said about you is not true?"

"O.K. O.K. then, the Chief did get frightened and jump overboard. But that wasn't my fault."

"When did this happen?"

"During the regatta. You must know that as well as I do. I was with him because he thought I could sail. He wanted to win, you see. And when that squall came up and I leaned over the railing to act as counterweight, he must have thought we were going to capsize and so he let out a yell and jumped into the water. And I—well, all I could do was to go on."

He looked gloomily at Jensen.

"If only I'd kept my mouth shut, everything would have been all right. But I thought it was a funny story. And then I got depressed when I found I was getting nice jobs because they wanted me out of the country. And then I couldn't keep quiet about that either, but what . . ."

He stopped suddenly and rubbed his nose.

"Don't take any notice of those stories. They're all just talk. My wife got well out of it and she does as she likes, doesn't she? And we're divorced now. I'm not complaining. Please don't think that."

After a brief pause he added:

"No, I'm not complaining."

"Show me the telegram."

The man stared in terror at Jensen.

"What telegram. I haven't . . .'

"Don't lie."

The man rose quickly and walked over to the window. He clenched his fists and beat them against each other.

"No," he said. "No, you won't trick me. I won't say anything more."

"Show me the telegram."

The man turned around. His fists were still clenched.

"It's no good. There is no telegram."

"Have you destroyed it?"

"I don't remember."

"What did it say?"

"I don't remember."

"Who signed it?"

"I don't remember."

"Why did you leave your job?"

"I don't remember."

"Where does your ex-wife live?"

"I don't remember."

"Where were you this time last week?"

"I don't remember."

"Were you here?"

"I don't remember."

The man in the dressing-gown was still standing with his back to the window and his fists clenched. His face was sweaty and his eyes frightened and childishly defiant. Jensen looked at him expressionlessly. About a minute later, he put his notebook into his pocket, picked up his hat and walked toward the door. Before he left the house, he said:

"What is Department Thirty-one?"

"I don't remember."

When he drove into the factory town, it was a quarter past eleven. He stopped at the police station and called the head of the Civil Patrol.

"Yes, they're divorced. Find out her address. Drive straight there and look at the diploma. If it isn't intact, take it with you."

"Right."

"It's urgent. I'll wait here."

"Right."

"One more thing."

"Yes?"

"He received a telegram yesterday or this morning. Send a man to get a copy."

"Right."

The police station was large and dismal with yellow brick walls and plastic curtains. At the back was a counter and behind that a row of cells with polished grids. Several of them were already occupied. Behind the counter sat a policeman in green uniform leafing through a file of reports.

Jensen sat down by the window and looked out over the empty silent square. The yellow smoke seemed to filter out all warmth from the sun and the light was flat and lifeless. The stench from the factory was appalling.

"Does it always smell like this?"

"It's worse on weekdays," said the constable.

Jensen nodded.

"You get used to it. The gases are said to be harmless, but my theory is that people get depressed by it. Lots commit suicide."

"Oh yes."

Fifty minutes later the telephone rang.

"She was very obliging," said the head of the Civil Patrol. "Showed it to me at once."

"And?"

"It was quite undamaged. Both pages there."

"Was there anything to show that it had been exchanged or renewed?"

"The signatures weren't recent anyhow. The ink wasn't fresh."

"Did you go into the apartment?"

"No. She got it. Obliging, as I said. It was almost as if I were expected. A very elegant lady, by the way."

"And the telegram?"

"I've sent a man to the post office."

"Recall him."

"You don't want a copy?"

"No."

Jensen paused. Then he said:

"It doesn't seem to have anything to do with the case."

"Inspector Jensen?"

"Just one small thing. One of my men was posted outside the building where she lives."

"Oh yes. Anything else?"

"The Chief of Police has been inquiring for you."

"Did he leave a message?"

"No."

The traffic on the highway had thickened and in many places there were cars parked off the side of the road. In most cases, the owners were busy polishing their cars, but many had taken out the seats and were sitting at small folding tables next to their cars. On the tables were portable television sets and pre-packed meals like those sold in automats. Nearer the city, the streams of vehicles became more troublesome, and when Jensen reached the center of the city, it was already ten to five.

The city was still deserted. The soccer season was in full swing and those who were not busy with their cars were indoors. Soccer matches nowadays were only televised. They were played without spectators in large heated television studios. The teams consisted of full-time players, among them many foreigners, but in spite of the fact that the standard was said to be very high, interest in the matches had declined. Jensen seldom looked at them, but on the other hand he always had the television switched on when he was home. He guessed that many others did the same.

During the hour that had just gone by, he had felt

increasingly exhausted and several times had almost blacked out. He realized that this was due to hunger and he stopped at an express food counter, where he bought a cup of hot water, a little plastic bag of clear soup powder and a portion of cheese.

As he waited for the soup powder to dissolve, he took out his notebook and wrote: Number 7, journalist, unmarried, 58 years old, left at his own request.

Although he drank the soup scalding hot, it was already half-past five when he got into the car again, and as he drove west dusk began to fall.

Six hours to go before midnight.

25

The street was narrow and frugally lit. It was bordered by an avenue of trees, and on each side were buildings on different levels. The district was not far from the center of the city. It had been built about forty years earlier and was chiefly inhabited by officials, who had presumably saved it from being turned into a standard development.

Jensen parked his car, crossed the street and rang the bell. No lights showed in the windows and no one came to the door.

He went back to the car, sat behind the wheel and studied his list and notebook. Then he put them back into his pocket, looked at his watch again, switched out the light in the car and waited.

Fifteen minutes later, a small man in a velour hat and a gray speckled overcoat came along the sidewalk. He unlocked the door and went in. Jensen waited until he saw lights go on behind the blinds. Then he crossed the street again and pressed the bell.

The man came to the door at once. He was simply and correctly dressed and his appearance matched his age. His face was thin and his gaze behind his glasses friendly and inquiring.

Jensen showed his badge.

"Jensen," he said. "Chief Inspector for the Sixteenth Division. I'm carrying out an investigation which concerns your former post and place of employment."

"Please come in," said the man, stepping to one side.

The room was quite big. Two walls were lined with shelves of books, papers and journals. By the window stood a desk with a telephone and typewriter on it, and in the middle of the floor stood a low circular smoking table and three armchairs. The light came from a rotary lamp on the desk and a plastic globe above the chairs and table.

The moment Jensen entered the room, his whole demeanor altered. His movements changed and so did his look. He gave the impression that he was about to do something he had done innumerable times before.

"Please do sit down."

Jensen sat down and took out his pen and notebook.

"In what way can I help you?"

"Some information."

"Naturally, I am at your service. If it is within my power to help."

"When did you leave your job?"

"At the end of the month of October last year."

"You had worked in the concern for a long time?"

"Relatively. To be more definite, fifteen years and four months."

"Why did you leave?"

"Let us say that I felt a desire to return to private life. I left the company at my own request, by handing in my resignation in the usual way."

The man's attitude was watchful, his voice subdued and tuneful.

"May I offer you anything? A cup of tea? Or?"

Jensen shook his head lightly.

"Where are you working at the moment?"

"I am financially independent and do not have to work for my living."

"What do you do?"

"I devote most of my time to reading."

Jensen looked around. The orderliness of the room was marked. Despite the number of books, journals and papers, everything looked neat and tidy, to the point of pedantry.

"When you left your job, did you receive a kind of diploma, or perhaps I should say a testimonial?"

"Yes, that is correct."

"Have you still got it?"

"I presume so. Would you like to see it?"

Jensen did not reply. For a full minute he sat quite still, without looking at the man. Then he said:

"Do you admit to sending an anonymous threatening letter to the management of the concern?"

"When is this supposed to have happened?"

"About this time last week."

The man had pulled up his trouser legs and crossed his legs. He was sitting with his left elbow on the arm of the chair and was slowly stroking his lower lip with his forefinger.

"No," he said calmly, "I do not admit that."

Jensen opened his mouth to say something, but changed his mind. Instead he looked at his watch. It said 7.11 p.m.

"I presume I am not the first person you have talked to

on this matter. How many people have you . . . questioned already?"

His tone of voice was more lively.

"About ten," said Jensen.

"Company people, all of them?"

"Yes."

"Then you must have had to endure a great many stories and smutty tales. Slander. Half-truths, peevishness, insinuations. And falsified accounts."

Jensen said nothing.

"The whole building is positively seething with such things, I gather," said the man.

"But then perhaps it's like that in most places," he added thoughtfully.

"What appointment did you hold during your time with the concern?"

"I was employed as a cultural journalist. The same appointment, as you call it, all the time."

"Then you are well versed in the company's organization and activities?"

"To some extent. Were you thinking of anything special?"

"Do you know anything about something called Department Thirty-one?"

"Yes."

"Do you know what it dealt with?"

"I should. I belonged to Department Thirty-one for fifteen years and four months."

After a minute or so of silence, Jensen said as if in passing:

"Do you admit to sending an anonymous threatening letter to the management of the concern?"

The man ignored the question.

"Department Thirty-one, or the Special Department, as it was also called, is the most important department in the company."

"I have heard this. What does it do?"

"Nothing," said the man. "Nothing whatsoever."

"Explain."

The man rose and got a piece of paper and a pencil from the scrupulously tidy desk. He sat down, placed the piece of paper exactly in line with the pattern on the table and put the pencil along the upper edge of the paper. Then he looked straight at his visitor.

"Yes," he said. "I shall explain."

Jensen looked at the time. 7.29. His respite had shrunk to four and a half hours.

"Are you in a hurry?"

"Yes."

"Then I'll try to make myself brief. You asked what the Special Department did, didn't you?"

"Yes."

"I have already given you a comprehensive answer. Nothing. The more one expands on that reply, the less comprehensive it becomes. Unfortunately. Do you follow me?"

"Of course not. We must hope that perhaps you will come to understand. Otherwise we run the risk of arriving at a deadlock."

The man fell silent for thirty seconds and during that time his attitude underwent certain changes. When he spoke he seemed weaker and more uncertain in some way, but also more committed than before.

"The simplest way is probably to tell you about myself.

I grew up in an intellectual home and was educated in the humanist tradition. My father was a university lecturer and I myself spent some years at the Academy. The Academy of the days when it possessed a humanities faculty in fact, not only in name. Do you fully realize what that implies?"

"No."

"I cannot explain everything. That would take much too long. It is possible that you have forgotten the meaning of the terms I use, but you must have heard them some time. It follows that you'll gradually understand their meaning and context."

Jensen put down his pen and listened.

"As I said before, I became a writer on cultural matters, at first because I didn't think I was capable of becoming an author. I was, quite simply, not suited to that, although writing was absolutely necessary to me. That was almost my only sorrow."

Pause. Light rain beat against the window.

"I worked for many years as a cultural editor on a privately owned daily newspaper. Not only information on art, literature, music and so on was to be found in its columns, but also on controversial subjects. For me, and for several others, these debates were perhaps the most important. They covered a very wide field and touched on practically every event in our society. They were often severely critical and remote from most points of view, and contributions were particularly well thought out."

Jensen made a movement.

"Stop," said the man, raising his right hand. "I think I know what you're going to say. Yes, it is quite correct to

say they disturbed people, that quite often they dismayed
them, disappointed them and frightened them. They never
attempted to follow the herd, whether they concerned
institutions, ideas or individuals. We, that is myself and
several others, considered this was right."

Jensen completed the movement and looked at his
watch. 7.45.

"It is said," said the man thoughtfully, "that criticism
and violent attacks on some occasion broke someone to
the extent that the person in question committed suicide."

There was silence for a few seconds. The rain could still
be heard.

"Some of us were called cultural radicals, but of course
we were all radicals, irrespective of our papers being
privately owned or socialist. I, on my part, however, did
not realize this until much later. On the other hand,
politics was not one of those things in which I took much
interest. Generally speaking, I did not trust our politicians.
Their qualities seemed to me inadequate, on both a human
and an educational level."

Jensen drummed lightly on the edge of the table with
his fingers.

"I see that you wish me to come to the point," the other
man said sorrowfully. "Well, another factor which I dis-
trusted even more wholeheartedly and consistently was
our weekly press. In my opinion, it had for a long time
done nothing but the utmost harm. In fact it naturally
filled a need of the time and should have been allowed to
live, but there was indeed no reason why it should have
been allowed to live in peace. I devoted much of my time

to attacking its so-called ideology, to dissecting and destroying it. I did this in many articles and in a controversial book."

He smiled a very small smile.

"That was a work which did not make me popular among those who cherished that kind of publication. I remember that I was called Public Enemy Number One of the weekly press. That was a long time ago now."

The man stopped and made some diagrammatical sketches on the piece of paper. The pencil lines were fine and finicky. He seemed to have a very light touch.

"Well, let us bow to the demands of time and make a long and involved story short and simple. The structure of society began to change, at first slowly and imperceptibly, then at a tremendous speed. Welfare and social equality began to be mentioned more and more, until both these phenomena were considered inextricably united and in all respects dependent on one another. At first nothing alarming happened, the housing problem was solved, crime declined, juvenile delinquency was beginning to be overcome. Simultaneously, the long-awaited moral reactionaries appeared, as punctual as the Ice Age. Nothing essentially disturbing, as I said. Only a few of us were suspicious. I presume you know what happened after that as well as I do."

Jensen did not reply. A new and strange sensation had begun to take possession of him. It was a sense of isolation and detachment, as if he and the little man with the glasses were enclosed in a plastic dome or in a glass case in some museum.

"The most significant effect on us, naturally, was that all publishing began to be consolidated under one roof, that company after company and paper after paper were sold to the same concern, always with the necessity of financial remuneration as to the fundamental motive. Everything went well, to such an extent that anyone who criticized anything began to feel like the famous dog that howled at the moon. Even people considered farsighted began to think that it was beggarly to arouse discussion on questions on which there was really only one viewpoint. I thought quite differently, never mind if this were perhaps due to defiance and monomania. A small number of us engaged in cultural activities, as the term was in those days, reacted in the same way."

There was complete silence in the room. The sounds from outside had ceased.

"The newspaper for which I worked was also drawn into the concern, of course. Exactly when this happened I do not remember. At the time, an apparently endless series of take-overs and combines was occurring, and nothing much was either written or said about it. My department had already shrunk more and more. Finally it was abandoned altogether, considered unnecessary. In practice, this meant that I was left without means of support, as were a number of colleagues on other papers and certain free-lance writers. For some reason it was only the most stubborn and controversial who could not find new jobs. The reason for this I did not understand until much later. Excuse me, I must get something to drink. What about you?"

Jensen shook his head. The man rose and disappeared through a door which presumably led to the kitchen. He returned with a glass of mineral water, drank a little and put the glass down.

"Anyhow, they'd never have been able to turn me into a sportswriter or a T.V. reviewer."

He lifted the glass a fraction, apparently to make sure that it had not left a mark on the table.

"A month or two went by and the future did not look particularly bright. Then one day, to my astonishment, I was invited to this great company to discuss the possibility of a job."

He paused again. Jensen checked the time. 8.05. After a moment's hesitation, he said:

"Do you admit to sending an anonymous threatening letter to the management of the concern?"

"No, no, not yet," said the man irritably.

He drank.

"I went there full of skepticism and was faced with the management of the time, in other words practically the same men as today. They were extremely courteous and the suggestion they made was nothing short of outstanding. I still remember how it was put."

The man laughed.

"Not because I have a good memory, but because I wrote it all down. They said that free discussion must not be allowed to die, and its perpetrators must not be allowed to become idle. That even if society were on its way to fulfilment, there would always be events to be debated. That free discussion—even if it were superfluous—was part of the primary assumptions of the ideal state. That existing culture, whatever form it might take, should be preserved and retained for posterity. Finally they said that the concern, now it had taken on the responsibility of such a large section of the country's vital publicity, was also prepared to take on the responsibility for cultural discussion as well. That they were planning the country's first comprehensive and completely unhampered cultural journal, employing the best writers."

The man seemed to become even more excited by his subject. He tried to catch Jensen's eye and hold it.

"They treated me very well. They made several respectful references to my frequently expressed views on the weekly press, shook me by the hand as if it were a ping-pong match and said they were delighted at the prospect of being able to refute my views. Finally they offered me a concrete proposal."

He sat in silence for a moment, looking absorbed in his own thoughts.

"Censorship," he said. "There's no official censorship in this country, is there?"

Jensen shook his head.

"And yet, I should say that the censorship here is more ruthless and more consistent than it could ever be in a police state. Why? Naturally because it is carried out privately and is quite unimpeded, using methods that are legally unassailable. Because, not the right to censor, please note, but the practical possibility of doing so, lies with people—whether officials or individuals—who are convinced that their decision is just and to everyone's benefit. And because the majority of people in fact also believe in this insane doctrine, and as a result act as censors themselves as long as there are opportunities."

He glanced at Jensen, as if checking that his audience was really with him.

"Everything is censored, the food we eat, the newspapers we read, the television programs we look at and the radio programs we listen to. Even the soccer matches are censored. I understand that incidents in which a player is hurt or grosser fouls are committed are cut out. All this is done for the good of the people. Developments in this direction were noticeable very early."

He drew a few more geometrical figures on his piece of paper.

"We who were occupied with cultural debates noticed this tendency a long time ago, though it first appeared in connection with something which did not really concern us. The most obvious of these symptoms occurred in the judicial system. It began with the official secrets acts being applied more and more rigorously. The army managed to persuade the lawyers and the politicians that all petty matters were vital to the security of the state. Then we noticed that other cases were also more and more often being held behind locked doors—a procedure I've always considered doubtful and objectionable, even if the accused happens to be a sex maniac. Finally, practically every minor trial took place out of reach of the public. The motive was always the same; to protect the individual from offensive, inflammatory or frightening facts, which might in some way influence his peace of mind. Simultaneously it became evident—I remember to this day the surprise with which I first noticed it—that diverse fairly highly placed officials were given the right to declare investigations and affairs connected with their own administrative duties secret. The most absurd inessentials such as reports on where a local authority should dump its rubbish and similar matter were made secret, without anyone doing anything about it. And within those concerns controlled by private capitalism, especially in the publishing world, censorship was exercised even more inflexibly.

Rarely from ill-will or malice, but on the grounds of something called moral responsibility."

He drank the rest of the mineral water.

"The moral qualities of the people who possessed the power to do this, we shall naturally keep very quiet about."

Jensen looked at the time. 8.17.

"The moment the Trade Union movement and the private employers achieved complete unity, a concentration of power without precedent was created. Organized opposition vanished of its own accord."

Jensen nodded

"There was no one to oppose. All problems had been solved, even the housing shortage and the parking problem. Everyone was materially better off, fewer children were born out of wedlock, crime declined. The only people who might oppose or criticize this phantom political combine, which had brought about this economic and moral miracle, were a handful of suspicious professional critics, such as I. People who could be expected to ask a great many awkward, meaningless questions. At what expense had this material wealth been won? Why were fewer children born out of wedlock? Why had crime decreased? And so on."

"To the point," said Jensen.

"Of course, to the point," the man said dryly. "The concrete proposal I received was certainly tempting. The concern was planning this formidable journal. This was to be written and edited by the best and most explosive and dynamic cultural personalities in the country. I remember the phraseology exactly. I was considered to be in this category, and I cannot deny that I was flattered. They showed me the list of editorial staff. I was astounded, for the people they had gathered together, about twenty-five of them, formed what I was at that time prepared to call the intellectual élite of the country. We were to have every possible resource at our disposal. You can imagine my astonishment."

Jensen looked indifferently at him.

"Naturally there were certain conditions. The paper must preferably pay its way. That was, after all, one of the fundamental doctrines. The other was that everyone must be protected from evil. Well, to be able to pay for itself, the paper had to be planned very thoroughly. Before it did that, a series of market research investigations had to be made. We could reckon on producing a considerable number of fully tested dummy editions. Nothing was to be left to chance. As far as the content and subject matter were concerned, we were to be given a free hand during the testing time, as well as later when the paper was put on the open market."

He smiled a bitter smile.

"They also said that one of their fundamental principles was that new projects such as this must be shrouded in complete secrecy. Otherwise someone, God knows who, might steal the whole idea. They pointed out that it had taken years, for example, to find the right form for a certain horror publication in the company's ordinary production. This was to prove that it paid to make haste slowly and absolutely discreetly to achieve perfection. Finally they put the contract in front of me. It was astonishingly advantageous. I was to be allowed, within reasonable limits, to state my own salary. The sum we agreed on was to be accounted for in such a way that everything I wrote would be entered and paid for. Even if the total fees did not cover the previously arranged sum, it would be paid all the same. Of course, an imbalance could occasionally occur this way. I could technically be in debt to the company or vice-versa. Then it was up to me to see that the balance was restored. Should I be in debt, I could produce more material, and should it be the other way about, I could rest. Otherwise the contract contained only a number of routine statements. I could be dismissed for misconduct or if I deliberately sabotaged the concern. I was not allowed to leave my job without having settled any eventual debts with the company, and several other things of that nature."

The man fingered his pencil but without moving it.

"I signed. The agreement gave me a much higher income than I had ever had before. Later it appeared that all the others had signed similar contracts. A week later I began work in the Special Department."

Jensen made an attempt to say something but stopped.

"The official name was the Special Department. Department Thirty-one came later. We were put on the thirty-first floor, the top one in the building. The offices there had no doubt originally been meant as some kind of storeroom or attic. Practically no one knew they existed. The elevators did not go up there and the only access to them was via a narrow spiral iron staircase. Neither were there any windows, only a couple of skylights in the roof. The idea of putting us there was twofold, we were told. Partly so that we could have complete peace to work in and partly because it would be easier to maintain absolute secrecy during the planning period. We had different working hours from the rest of the staff. At the time, this all seemed quite plausible. Does that surprise you?"

Jensen did not reply.

"So we began to work, at first under considerable strain. Just imagine a dozen or so individualists, with opposing wills and no obvious common denominator. We had as an editor a complete illiterate who later was appointed to a very prominent position in the concern. I can enrich your stock of stories by telling you that he was said to have received senior journalistic posts because he, like the Chief and the publisher, is word-blind. However, he made no fuss at all. The first dummy edition was not printed for eight months, mostly because the technical side of production had been strangely dilatory. It was a good and bold issue and to our undisguised astonishment, it was extremely well received by the management. Although many of the articles were critical of most things, the weekly press included, no comment was made on the content. They only advised us to adjust a number of technical details and first and foremost to increase the rate of production. Before we could guarantee a new issue every two weeks, it was impossible to think in terms of regular publication. Even this sounded plausible."

He looked at Jensen in a friendly way.

"It took two years before we, with all our resources and the increasingly clumsy setting and printing, succeeded in publishing two issues a month. The paper was printed all the time. We produced ten dummy runs every issue. They were filed for the records; the demand for discretion meant that under no circumstances were we allowed to take a copy out of the offices. Well, when we had gotten so far, the management seemed satisfied, almost delighted, and they said that all that was needed now was to give the paper a new layout, a modern form which would enable it to stand up to the steep competition on the open market. And believe it or not, it was not until this reorganization, which was carried out by a very peculiar group of people, had gone on for eight months without visible results, that . . ."

"That what?" said Jensen

"That we at least began to realize the full extent of what they were doing. When we began to protest, they appeased us by printing larger dummy editions, about five hundred copies which, it was said, would be sent out to all the daily papers and more important quarters. Gradually we noticed this was a complete lie, but it took time. It was not until we had definitely established that the name of the paper had never been mentioned and that the contents had not been commented on, that we really realized that the editions had never been distributed at all. That it had only been used as a correlation, or rather an indication of what and how one should not write. We received only our usual ten copies. Since then . . ."

"Yes?"

"Since then this unprecedented lunacy has continued, much as before. Day after day, month after month, year after year, this country's cultural élite, the last of their kind, have sat in those ghostlike offices and with decreasing enthusiasm, have put out a paper, which, despite everything, is still the only one in the country worthy of its name. And which is never published. Meanwhile they have found hundreds of different excuses why it should not be. The final form was not acceptable, the production rate was too low, the capacity of the presses was not great enough, and so on. The only thing they never find fault with is the content."

He knocked on the edge of the table with his right index finger.

"And the content could have changed a great deal. It could have woken people up before it was too late. It could have saved many people, quite simply. I know that that is true."

The man suddenly raised his hand as if to interrupt.

"I know, you were going to ask why we didn't leave. The answer is very simple. We could not."

"Explain."

"Certainly. Our contracts were so drawn up that we were hopelessly in debt to the concern. After the first six months alone, I owed the company more than half the money I had earned. After five years this sum had increased four-fold. After fifteen it was astronomical, at least for people in ordinary financial circumstances. This debt was a so-called technical debt. We received routine notes about it. But no one demanded that we actually pay the sum. Not until the moment arrived when we wanted to leave Department Thirty-one."

"But you yourself left?"

"Yes, thanks to a unique situaton. I inherited a fortune, quite unexpectedly. Although it was quite a considerable one, almost half of it went to settling the company's claim. A claim which, with the help of various tricks, they succeeded in increasing right up to the moment I wrote out the check. But I was free. Had it cost me the entire fortune, I'd have torn myself free. When I'd done it, I suppose I could have stolen to get money."

He laughed.

"Theft is a discipline with few practitioners today, isn't it?"

"Admit that you . . ."

The man interrupted at once.

"Do you understand the implications of what I have just said? This was murder, an intellectual murder, far more loathsome and distasteful than physical murder. The murder of innumerable ideas, the murder of opinions, of freedom of speech. Premeditated first-degree murder of them all, to give people guaranteed peace of mind, to make them disposed to swallow uncritically all the tripe that's stuffed into them. Do you see, to spread indifference without opposition, forcibly injecting poison after first making sure there is neither doctor nor serum available."

He said this violently and swiftly and went on almost at once, without pausing for breath.

"You'll protest of course that we were all so well off, except the nine who went mad or took their own lives. And that it cost the concern a great deal of money to publish a paper that was never published. Bah! Money, to them, with their tax lawyers working for the tax authorities at the same time . . ."

He stopped and became quite calm.

"I apologize for resorting to that sort of argument. Yes, of course I admit it. You knew that I would from the very beginning, anyhow. But not only did I want to make some things clear first, but it was also an experiment on my own part. I wanted to see how long I could avoid admitting it."

The man smiled and said in an off-hand manner:

"I lack talent when it comes to not telling the truth."

"Explain your motive."

"When I succeeded in breaking free, I wanted to draw some attention to the matter. But I soon saw that any hope of writing something and getting it published was quite fruitless. Finally I thought that perhaps there might still be some reaction to brutal and sensational events. So I sent the letter. I was, of course, wrong. On that particular day, I had succeeded in acquiring permission to visit one of my ex-colleagues in the mental hospital opposite the concern's main building. I watched the police barricade the area and the fire trucks drive up and how the whole building was emptied. But not a word was printed or said about the matter."

"You are prepared to repeat your confession in the presence of witnesses? And sign a statement?"

"Of course," said the man absently. "Anyhow you should have no difficulty in finding all the material evidence you might need. Here at home."

Jensen nodded. The man rose and went over to the shelves.

"I too, shall produce some material evidence. This is a copy of the paper that doesn't exist. The last one produced before I left."

The paper was very dignified. Jensen leafed through it.

"Although the years broke us, we hadn't become so toothless that they dared let us go," said the man. "We dealt with all manner of questions. Nothing was taboo."

The contents of the paper were astonishing. Jensen's face was absolutely expressionless. He stopped and stared at a reference to the physical aspects of the falling birth rate and sexual impoverishment. Two large pictures of naked women flanked the text. They apparently represented two different types. One reminded him of the photographs in the sealed envelopes he had found in the editor's desk, a flat, straight, well-fed body with narrow hips and shaved or scarcely visible pubic hair. The other was a photograph of Number 4, the woman in whose apartment, twenty-four hours earlier, he had leaned against the doorpost, drinking a glass of water. She was standing upright, relaxed, her arms hanging free and her feet slightly apart. She had large dark nipples, broad hips and a curved stomach. From her loins an abundance of black hair grew over the lower part of her abdomen. Despite this, her sex organ was quite visible on the picture; it seemed to protrude from the angle between her thighs.

"That's a recent picture," commented the man. "We wouldn't accept anything else, but it was hard to get. That type is said to be even more uncommon now than earlier."

Jensen leafed on. He closed the paper and looked at the time. 9.06.

"Get your toilet things and come with me," he said.

The little man in glasses nodded.

"I have one more thing to confess."

"What?"

"They'll get an identical letter tomorrow at the same time. I'd just been to mail it when you came."

"Why?"

"I don't give in easily. But this time they probably won't bother about it at all."

"What do you know about explosives?"

"Less than what the managing director knows about Hegel."

"Which means?"

"Which means absolutely nothing whatsoever. I have never even been in the service. I was a pacifist even in those days. If I had a complete stock of army supplies at my disposal, I still wouldn't be able to put together something which would explode. Do you believe me?"

"Yes."

Half way to the Sixteenth Division station, Inspector Jensen said:

"Did it ever occur to you to blow up the building?"

The man did not reply until they swung in through the entrance of the yard.

"Yes. If I'd been capable of constructing a bomb and if I could have been certain that no one was hurt, then perhaps I would have blown up the building. So it became a symbolic bomb, so to speak."

When the car had stopped, he mumbled, as if to himself:

"Now I've told it all, anyhow. To a policeman."

He turned to his companion and said:

"I suppose the trial won't be public?"

"I don't know," said Jensen.

He switched off the tape-recorder under the instrument panel and got out, went around the car and opened the door on the other side. He took the man in, went up to his room and called the head of the Civil Patrol.

"You've got the address?"

"Yes."

"Take two men and go there. Collect all the material evidence you can find. It's urgent."

"Right."

"One more thing."

"Yes."

"Send an interrogator down to isolation It's a confession."

"Right."

Then he looked at the clock. It was twenty-five to ten. There were two hours and twenty-five minutes left until midnight.

26

"Jensen? What have you been doing?"

"Completing the investigation."

"I've been trying to contact you for two days. Things have taken a new turn."

Jensen said nothing.

"Besides, what do you mean by completing?"

"The culprit has been found."

He heard the Chief of Police's heavy breathing.

"Has the person confessed?"

"Yes."

"Is it proven?"

"Yes."

"Tied up with the offense?"

"Yes."

The Chief of Police seemed to think.

"Jensen, the head of the concern must be told at once."

"Yes."

"You must do it. I think you ought to take him the news personally."

"Right."

"Perhaps it's just as well I didn't get hold of you earlier."

"I don't understand."

"The management of the concern contacted me yesterday. Via the Minister. They thought it best to abandon the investigation. They were even prepared to withdraw the charge."

"Why?'

"I got the impression that they thought the investigation had come to a dead end. And also that they were finding your methods troublesome, that you were fumbling about in the dark and only bringing unpleasantness to innocent and apparently quite prominent people."

"I see."

"The whole thing was very painful. But as I didn't really have much hope that you would succeed within the time, I felt bound to agree. The Minister asked me directly if I thought you had a chance. I was forced to answer no. But now . . ."

"Yes?"

"Now everything takes on quite a different perspective, as far as I can see."

"Yes. There's one more thing."

"What about?"

"The man has evidently written another threatening letter, identical to the first. It should arrive tomorrow."

"Is he harmless?"

"Probably."

"Well, if he isn't, then we're in the unique position of having detained the guilty man sixteen hours before the crime is committed."

Jensen said nothing.

"The most important thing at the moment is to inform

the head of the concern. You must get hold of him now, tonight. For your own sake."

"Right."

"Jensen?"

"Yes."

"You've done a good job. Good-bye."

Jensen let the receiver rest for less than ten seconds and then put it to his ear again. As he dialed the numbers, he could hear long drawn-out hysterical wails from the yard.

It took him five minutes to locate the head of the concern at one of his country places; after another five minutes he managed to contact the place. The person he spoke to was obviously a servant.

"The matter is important."

"The master's not to be disturbed."

"It's urgent."

"I can't do anything about it. He has had a fall."

"Is there a telephone in his bedroom?"

"Of course."

"Put me through."

"I'm sorry but I can't. He has had a fall . . ."

"I realize that. Let me speak to one of the family."

"Madam has gone out."

"When is she coming back?"

"I don't know."

Jensen put down the receiver and looked at the clock. It was a quarter past ten.

The cheese and soup made themselves known in the form of heartburn, and when he had removed his coat, he went into the cloakroom and drank a mug of bicarbonate.

The country place lay twenty miles or so to the east, by

a lake and in an area of untouched country. Jensen drove quickly with the sirens on and covered the stretch in less than twenty-five minutes.

He stopped a little way from the house and waited. When the man from the Civil Patrol came out of the dark, he rolled down the window.

"There's been an accident?"

"Well—accident. Anyhow, he seems to be in bed. But I haven't seen a doctor. It happened some hours ago."

"Be specific."

"Well, it must have been about . . . anyhow it was at dusk."

"Do you know what happened?"

"Yes, exactly. I was in a good place. I couldn't be seen myself but could see the whole of the terrace in front of the house and into the room on the ground floor, as well as the stairs to his bedroom. And the door up there."

"What happened?"

"They've got guests. With small children—for the week-end, I think."

He fell silent.

"Yes?"

"Small children—perhaps they're foreigners," said the policeman thoughtfully. "Well, the children were playing on the terrace and he was sitting with some of his guests in the big room, drinking something. Liquor, I think, but only a moderate amount, as far as I could make out."

"To the point."

"Well, then a badger came up on the terrace."

"And?"

"It was a stray. Well, the children began to cry and the

badger couldn't get down again. There's a balustrade around the terrace and the animal was running all over the place. The children cried more and more loudly."

"Yes."

"There were no servants about. And no menfolk except him. And me, of course. He got up then, and went out on the terrace and looked at the badger running about. The children were screaming by then. At first he hesitated and then he went up to the badger and kicked at it to make it go away. The badger swung its head around and sort of nudged his foot. Then it found the opening and ran away."

"And the Chief?"

"Well, he went back into the house and didn't sit down, but walked slowly upstairs. And then I saw him opening the door to his room, but he crumpled up just inside the doorway. He seemed to be groaning and calling for his wife. She rushed up and led him to the bed. They shut the door, but I think she helped him undress. She went in and out once or twice, with different things, cups, perhaps a thermometer. I couldn't see all that well."

"Was he bitten by the animal?"

"We-ell, not exactly bitten. More likely scared I should say. Funny . . ."

"What?"

"The badger. Funny at this time of year, I meant. Badgers usually hibernate in the winter. I remember that from a nature program on television, the kind they used to show."

"Avoid superfluous information."

"Yes, sir."

"You can return to normal duties from now on."

"Yes, sir."

The man fingered his binoculars.

"It's been a very odd job, if I may say so."

"Your manner of reporting leaves a great deal to be desired."

"Yes, sir."

Jensen walked up to the house and was let in by a servant girl. A clock in the house struck eleven. He stood with his hat in his hand and waited. Five minutes later the wife of the Chief appeared.

"At this time?" she said haughtily. "And my husband has had a bad accident and is in bed."

"The matter is important. And urgent."

She went up one flight of stairs. A few minutes later she came back and said:

"If you use the telephone over there, you can speak to him. But only for a short time."

Jensen lifted the receiver.

The Chief sounded exhausted, but his voice was firm and resonant.

"Oh, yes. And you've arrested him?"

"Detained."

"Where is he?"

"For the next three days in the Sixteenth Division cells."

"Splendid. Naturally the poor man is deranged."

Jensen said nothing.

"Has anything else arisen from the investigation?"

"Nothing of interest."

"Splendid. I wish you good evening."

"There is one other thing."

"Make it brief. You've come very late and I've had a strenuous day."

"Before the man was detained, he said he mailed another anonymous letter."

"Oh, yes. Do you know what's in it?"

"According to him, it is exactly the same as the last one."

The silence went on for so long that Jensen began to think the conversation was at an end. When the Chief eventually spoke, his voice had changed.

"Then he's threatening another bomb attack?"

"Evidently."

"Could he have had the opportunity of smuggling in and hiding an explosive charge in the building?"

"It seems unlikely."

"But the possibility cannot be entirely ruled out?"

"Naturally not. However, it can be considered extremely unlikely."

The Chief's tone of voice had been thoughtful. After a pause of thirty seconds, he concluded the conversation by saying:

"Obviously the man must be insane. The whole thing seems most unpleasant. But if any measures are to be taken, they can hardly be carried out until tomorrow. I wish you good evening."

Jensen drove slowly and by midnight he still had some miles to cover before reaching the city. Soon after that, he was overtaken by a large black car. It looked like the Chief's, but he could not be certain.

It was two o'clock in the morning before he reached home.

He was tired and hungry and did not have the feeling

of relative satisfaction he usually felt when a case was closed.

He undressed in the dark, went out to the kitchen and poured out a stiff dose of spirits. Then he emptied the glass in one draught, standing naked by the sink, rinsed it out and went to bed.

Chief Inspector Jensen fell asleep immediately. His last conscious impression was of a sense of isolation and dissatisfaction.

27

Jensen was wide awake the moment he opened his eyes. Something had woken him, but he did not know what. It could hardly have been an external event, such as the telephone or a cry. More likely his sleep had been penetrated by a thought which had been as sharp and clear as a flash of lightning, but which immediately disintegrated as he opened his eyes.

He lay still on his back in bed and stared at the ceiling. A quarter of an hour later he got up and went into the kitchen. The electric clock said five to seven and it was Monday.

Jensen took a bottle of mineral water from the refrigerator, poured it out and remained standing by the window with the glass in his hand. The view below was gray and scrubby and desolate. He drank the mineral water, went into the bathroom and filled the bath, took off his pajamas and got in. He lay in the water until it began to cool, then he got up, and took a shower, towelled himself and dressed.

He did not bother to read the morning papers but ate three biscuits with his honey-water. They had no noticeable effect and his hunger increased, tormenting, wild, and churning.

Although he kept to a moderate speed on the highway, he nearly overshot a red light at the bridge and had to brake sharply. The cars behind hooted reproachfully in unison.

At exactly half-past eight he went into his office and two minutes later the telephone rang.

"Did you find him?"

"On the telephone. He was indisposed. In bed."

"What was wrong with him? Was he ill?"

"He'd been frightened by a badger."

The Chief of Police said nothing for a while and Jensen listened as usual to his uneven breathing.

"Well, it can't have been all that serious, anyhow. Early this morning, both he and his cousin left by air for some congress abroad."

"And?"

"I didn't call because of that. But to tell you your troubles are over for this time. I presume you've all the statements?"

Jensen leafed through the papers on his desk.

"Yes," he said.

"The Public Prosecutor has considered the matter pressing. His people are coming to get your man in about ten minutes and are taking him to the examination prison. Send the reports and statements connected with the case."

"Right."

"As soon as the Prosecutor has accepted responsibility for the man, you can close the case and note it down in the case-book. Then both you and I can happily forget it all."

"Right."

"Good, Jensen. Good-bye."

The men from the Prosecutor's office arrived punctually. Jensen stood by his window, watching them take the man to the car. The man in the velour hat and gray speckled overcoat appeared untroubled and looked inquisitively around the concrete yard. There was nothing to see but hoses and buckets and a couple of sanitation men in sulphur-yellow rubber overalls.

Both the guards seemed to be taking their task very seriously. They had not put handcuffs on the man, nor were they holding his arms, but they closed in on him from either side and Jensen observed that one of them had his right hand in his overcoat pocket all the time. Presumably the man was new at the job.

Jensen remained standing by the window for a long time after the car had driven away. Then he sat down at his desk, took out his spiral notebook and read through his notes. Several times he stopped for long pauses or turned back the pages to something he had read before.

When the clock on the wall struck eleven short strokes, he put down the notebook and gazed at it for about ten minutes. Then he put the notebook into a brown envelope and sealed it. He wrote a number on the back and put it in the bottom drawer of the desk.

Chief Inspector Jensen rose and went down to the lunch-room, automatically acknowledging the greetings of the staff on the way.

He ordered a complete standard lunch, took his loaded tray and carried it over to a corner table which was always reserved for him. The lunch consisted of three slices of meat loaf, two fried onions, five watery potatoes and a limp lettuce leaf, all covered with a thick layer of white sauce. Also half a pint of homogenized milk, five slices of dry bread, a portion of vitaminized vegetable fat, a piece of processed cheese, a mug of black coffee, and soggy cake with fancy icing on top.

He ate slowly and systematically and absentmindedly as if the procedure really had nothing to do with him.

When he had finished, he picked his teeth thoroughly. Then he sat completely motionless, his back straight and his clenched fists resting on the edge of the table. He did not seem to be looking at anything in particular and people passing his table could not catch his eye.

After half an hour, he went up to his office and sat down at the desk. He leafed through the latest routine papers on suicide and alcoholism and pulled a report out of the heap. He tried to read it but was not very successful.

He was sweating copiously and his thinking processes were beginning to become undisciplined, breaking through the barriers in a way he seldom allowed them to.

The lunch had been too much for his ruined digestive system.

He put the report down and got up, crossed the corridor and went into the cloakroom.

Chief Inspector Jensen closed the door and thrust the first two fingers of his right hand down his throat and vomited. The contents of his stomach tasted sour and soon ceased to come up automatically.

He knelt down in front of the lavatory seat and held on to it, and as he retched he thought that anyone could come in through the door and shoot him from behind. If the person had a good revolver, the back of his head would be blown off and he would be thrown forward over the toilet and they would find him like that.

When his convulsions were over, his thoughts returned to their habitual channels.

After he had washed, he bathed the back of his neck and his wrists with cold water. Then he combed his hair, brushed down his jacket and returned to his office.

28

Jensen had just sat down when the telephone rang. He lifted the receiver and out of habit glanced at the clock. 1.08 p.m.

"Jensen?"

"Yes."

"They've got the letter, just as you said they would."

"Yes?"

"The managing director has just been in contact with me. He sounded hesitant and worried."

"Why?"

"As I said before, both of his superiors are abroad. So he's left with the entire responsibility over there and he doesn't seem to have received any specific instructions."

"Instructions for what?"

"What measures should be taken. He'd evidently not been told about the letter. It descended on him like a bomb, so to speak. I got the impression that he didn't even know that the culprit had been found."

"I see."

"He asked me time and time again if it really was a hundred percent certain that there was no explosive charge in the building. I told him that the risk of that being so seemed very small. But to guarantee something, what ever it is, a hundred per cent . . . can you do that?"

"No."

"In any case, he wants to have some men to help in case anything happens. We can hardly deny him that."

"I see."

The Chief of Police cleared his throat.

"Jensen?"

"Yes."

"There's no reason why you personally should go. You've had a strenuous week and the job is more or less a routine one this time. And also . . ."

He paused briefly.

"And also the managing director didn't sound exactly delighted at the prospect of meeting you again."

"Yes."

"Send out the same force as before. Your right-hand man is familiar with the case. Let him take over."

"Right."

"If you want to, of course, you can direct the operation from radio headquarters. You can use your own discretion on that."

"Right."

"Of course, this does not mean disapproval of you. I hope you realize that. But there's no reason why we shouldn't show a little flexibility when the opportunity arises."

"I see."

Jensen set off the alarm system as he gave instructions to the head of the Civil Patrol.

"Be discreet. Avoid all fuss."

"Yes, sir."

He put down the receiver and heard the bells ringing in the basement.

Ninety seconds later the vehicles left the yard. It was 1.12.

He remained where he was for a minute more and tried to concentrate his thoughts. Then he rose, walked the short way to radio headquarters. The policeman on duty at the control board rose and stood at attention. Jensen took his place.

"Where are you?"

"Two blocks away from the Trade Union Palace."

"Switch off the sirens when you've reached the square."

"Right."

Jensen's voice was calm and ordinary. He did not look at the clock. The schedule was fixed. The head of the Civil Patrol should be inside the building by 1.26.

"I just passed the square. I can see the building now."

"No uniformed men inside or in the immediate vicinity of the building."

"Right."

"Post the patrolmen three hundred yards from the building, half at each approach road."

"Right."

"Increase the distance between your vehicles."

"Done."

"Follow last week's schedule."

"Right."

"Contact me as soon as you've sized up the situation. I'll be here."

Jensen stared in silence at the instrument panel.

The building was one of the highest in the country and because of its position, could be seen from all parts of the city. One always saw it above oneself and from whichever direction one came, it seemed to form the terminus of the approach road. It was square and thirty floors high. On each façade were four hundred fifty windows and a white clock with red hands. The outer surface was of glazed tiles, dark blue below, getting lighter and lighter the higher they rose. As the head of the Ciivl Patrol looked at the building through the car window, it seemed to shoot out of the ground, like an enormous column growing in the cold cloudless spring sky. The building became enlarged and filled his field of vision.

"I'm there now. End of message."

"End of message."

Jensen looked at his watch. 1.27.

The radio operator switched on.

Jensen neither moved nor took his eyes off the wall clock. The second hand ate into the time with small rapid jerks.

It was completely silent in the room. Jensen's face was tense and concentrated, his pupils contracted and a fine network of lines appeared around his eyes. The operator looked intently at his superior.

1.34 ... 1.35 ... 1.36 ... 1.37 ...

The radio crackled. Jensen did not move.

"Inspector Jensen?"

"Yes."

"I've seen the letter. Definitely put together by the same person. Same kind of letters and everything. Only the paper is different."

"Go on."

"The man I spoke to, the managing director, was

extremely nervous. Obviously scared stiff something will happen while the top men are away."

"And?"

"They're evacuating the whole building, just as before. Four thousand, one hundred people. The evacuation has begun."

"Where are you?"

"Outside the main entrance. People are pouring out."

"The firemen?"

"Alerted. One fire engine. It'll do. Excuse me . . . I must organize the barriers now. I'll be back."

He heard the head of the Civil Patrol giving orders to someone. Then silence fell.

1.46. Jensen was still sitting in the same position. His expression remained unchanged.

The radio operator shrugged and suppressed a yawn.

1.52. The loudspeaker crackled.

"Inspector Jensen?"

"Yes."

"It's beginning to thin out. Went faster this time. These should be the last coming out now."

"The situation?"

"All's well. The barriers are a hundred per cent effective. Blaming damaged deep heating pipe. The fire engine is there already. Everything's going well."

The head of the Civil Patrol sounded calm and confident. His voice was relaxed, almost soothing.

"Lord, what a lot of people. Like an ant heap. They're all out now."

Jensen's eyes followed the second hand, around, around, around, 1.55.

The radio operator yawned.

"Lucky it's not raining," said the head of the Civil Patrol.

"Avoid unnec . . ."

Chief Inspector Jensen jerked and half rose to his feet.

"Has everyone left the building? Be exact."

"Yes, except for the little special department. It's supposed to be well protected and it's difficult to evacuate at such short . . ."

The pattern fell into place. He saw everything with crystal clarity as if in the light of a magnesium flash. Jensen sat down while the other man was speaking.

"Where are you?"

"Immediately outside . . ."

"Into the entrance hall. It's urgent."

Jensen knew what he had thought in that fraction of a second as he had awakened that morning.

"Yes, sir."

"Quick. The telephone. By the commissionaire's desk. Dial the number of Department Thirty-one. There's a list of numbers in front of you."

Silence. 1.56.

"The telephone—it's dead—the number . . ."

"The elevators?"

"The electricity system's switched off altogether—telephones and everything . . ."

"What about the stairs? How long?"

"Don't know. Ten minutes . . ."

"Are any of your men in the building?"

"Two, but only four floors up."

"Get them down. Don't reply. You've no time."

1.57.

"They're on their way down."

"Where's the fire engine?"

"Outside the main entrance. My men are coming now."

"Get the fire engine around the corner to the annex."

"Done."

1.58.

"Get yourself in a safe place. Behind the annex. Run."

Heavy crackling panting.

"Is the building empty?"

"Yes ... except those ... thirty-first ..."

"I know. Stand close to the wall, in the dead angle for protection against falling objects. Open your mouth. Think of your tongue. End of message."

1.59.

Jensen switched off.

"Sound the disaster alarm," he said to the radio operator. "Don't forget the helicopter service. It's urgent."

Chief Inspector Jensen rose to his feet and went into his office. He sat down at his desk and waited. He sat quite still and wondered whether the explosion would be audible as far away as this.